A TIN

MW01136131

Nick Ryan

A World War 3 Technothriller Action Event

035139

262960

Dedication:

For Ebony, with all my love and appreciation.
-Nick.

About the Series:

The WW3 novels are a chillingly authentic collection of action-packed combat thrillers that envision a modern war where the world's superpowers battle on land, air and sea using today's military hardware.

Each title is a 50,000-word stand-alone adventure that forms part of an ever-expanding series, with several new titles published every year.

Facebook: https://www.facebook.com/NickRyanWW3
Website: https://www.worldwar3timeline.com

Other titles in the collection:

- 'Charge to Battle'
- 'Enemy in Sight'
- 'Viper Mission'
- 'Fort Suicide'
- 'The Killing Ground'
- 'Search and Destroy'
- 'Airborne Assault'
- 'Defiant to the Death'
- 'A Time for Heroes'

The Fight for Germany

Once the Russian Army had captured Warsaw a
west in pursuit of NATOs shattered retreating f
seemed inevitable that Berlin would be the next capital
to the conquering victors.

But at the Polish border the Russians met unexpected sto
defense from the German troops hastily arrayed to protect the
Fatherland.

The bulk of Germany's armed forces were still mobilizing;
still gravitating from their bases across the country towards
their eastern border. The troops who met and blunted the
spearhead of the Russian attack during the first desperate
hours of the conflict were not elite; they were regular infantry
who had been rushed from their nearby billets as a stop-gap
measure.

Overhead, German Luftwaffe pilots flying Panavia
Tornados and Eurofighter Typhoons flew vital strike missions
against the Russians to forestall their seemingly inevitable
march into Germany, while on the ground Panzer units based
in the west of the country rushed eastwards to reinforce the
frontline.

Amongst those troops that were the first to meet the
Russian invaders were a rag-tag collection of American, British
and French units; some of them fresh and newly arrived to
Germany, and others who were the remnants from Warsaw's
ill-fated defense.

Russia's hopes of a swift march to Berlin began to grind to
a bloody halt in the muddy terrain around the towns of
Frankfurt an der Oder and Eisenhüttenstadt.

During the first twenty-four hours of grim, bitter fighting, a
ragged battlefront developed that stretched between the village
of Guben in the south of Germany all the way north to
Schwedt.

In the days that followed, Russia built up its armies, flying
reserve troops west to the border and beginning a relentless
artillery bombardment that would precede a hammer blow
strike designed to shatter NATO resistance and clear the road

rst frontal attack came, the Allies
ling ground but doggedly fighting

became a bloody stalemate even
clear superiority in troop and

:ted Allied resistance, Russian
the initiative along the German battlefront
to be regained – urgently. A second wave of attacks were
organized, designed to envelop the northern edge of the Allied
line. With one fell swoop, the Russians planned to outflank the
Americans and German positions and collapse the entire front.

Allied satellite intelligence sources caught wind of the
imminent Russian outflanking maneuver and issued an urgent
warning.

Suddenly the fight for Germany became a race to evacuate
civilians in the way of the planned Russian attack… and a rush
to gather a force strong enough to fend off the enemy advance
and then push them back into Poland.

*It was a do-or-die Allied plan, and the entire campaign began with
just one Company of American infantry on a desperate rescue mission…*

SCHWEDT
NORTH EASTERN GERMANY

Chapter 1:

They moved like dead men; their bodies coated with dust and grime, their feet shuffling, their minds near insensible with crushing fatigue as they wound their way through the town. Smoke hung thick in the air around the Stadtpfarrkirche St. Katharinen church, close to the heart of Schwedt. The church had been destroyed the day before by Russian artillery. Now all that remained was a charred ruin and a scatter of rubble which was strewn across the road the Company of American infantry were using to reach the battlefront.

The Americans were from Bravo Company, 4th Battalion, 6th Infantry Regiment and in the lead was Captain Hank Elway, the commander of the veteran unit. Elway had his eyes on the near horizon, watching billowing columns of black smoke rise into the battle haze as enemy artillery rounds pounded the Allied lines. Elway was new to the war, but not new to combat. He had joined the US Army as a teenager and had spent almost half his life on active duty. He and his men had arrived to the fight for Europe only three weeks earlier – but to Elway it seemed like a lifetime ago.

Elements of the 6th Infantry Regiment were part of the rag-tag collection of units hastily cobbled together by NATO command to defend the German border against the invading Russians while the bulk of the German Army was still mobilizing for action. The men from Bravo Company had been fighting on the frontlines for the past week. Now they were filing forward once again towards the eastern outskirts of Schwedt and marching straight into the jaws of a fresh hell as Russian artillery whipped itself into a frenzy.

Behind Elway followed the rest of the Company. Despite their fatigue they carried themselves with the calm easy confidence of combat warriors. Some of them were veterans; some of them were young soldiers seeing the gruesome atrocity of war for the first time.

At the end of the rubble-littered street two German Feldjägers (military police) armed with HK G36k assault rifles stood waiting beside an ATF Dingo. The MPs paid little attention to the Americans until they were within a few yards. Then the passenger-side door of the heavily armored MRAP (Mine-resistant ambush protected) vehicle swung open and a uniformed Bundeswehr officer in a clean uniform stepped down into the dust.

He was a young Lieutenant with a thatch of short blonde hair, a pale face and unnaturally red lips. He looked the column of Americans up and down and appeared unimpressed.

"You are Bravo Company, 4th Battalion, yes?" in his left hand he carried a handful of paperwork.

"That's right, bud," Hank Elway did not slow his step or give the German officer more than a glance. He just kept walking towards the battlefront, his boots crunching through the debris and dust.

The German junior officer looked alarmed. "Wait!" he barked, and the two Feldjägers reached urgently for their weapons in response to the strident command, without understanding the danger.

Hank Elway stopped and turned around slowly. His voice when he spoke was heavy with menace. He was exhausted; worn down by six days of combat and killing. He and his men had barely slept in the past week. They were unwashed, unshaven and covered in blood and grime and dust. They stank of sweat and stale piss, vomit and smoke.

"I have to tell you where your troops are required to search," the German Lieutenant pouted with the affront of an ignored petty official.

"I know where we're required to search," Elway's voice betrayed his rising frustration. He pointed into the distance at the billowing columns of black smoke that were being stabbed through with flashes of fiery explosions. "Wherever the fighting is fiercest."

The Company marched on, heading due east towards the Oder River that delineated the Germany-Poland border. The men following Elway walked in two columns seemingly oblivious to the pedantic German officer. The men's thoughts were on the mission ahead, and of survival. The midday sun was hot on their backs and the dust kicked up by their shuffling boots powdered their faces grey and filled their mouths with grit. Smoke skeins drifted across the street, carried along by the breeze while overhead the sky suddenly filled with a savage snarling howl of jet engines.

The men looked up in alarm as two Russian Su-25 'Frogfoot' close-support fighters burst through a cloud of black smoke and came screaming towards the center of the town at low altitude.

"Down! Everybody down!" Elway bellowed.

The soldiers scrambled off the road and hurled themselves down into the rubble as the two Russian jets flashed overhead. The Russian aircraft ignored the American infantry and instead banked sharply to the north, firing their wing-mounted rockets into a nearby grove of woods where Allied artillery had been positioned. The ground beneath Elway's men shuddered and shook through a series of deep rumbling explosions.

The 'Frogfoots' vanished as quickly as they had appeared, turning back to the east and retreating across the battlefront, chased by German SAMs. Elway heaved himself wearily to his feet.

"Reckon we're almost where we should be," the Company's First Sergeant, Joe Moon, searched the distant sky for a trace of the retreating Russian jets but could not find them in the swirling banks of smoke. The Sergeant was a stout man with huge muscled shoulders and the physique of a bull.

Elway grunted dutifully. The Captain was too tired and too hot to make the effort of conversation and so Moon turned his attention to the men instead, growling at them to pick up the pace, berating the laggers at the rear of the column and cajoling those closest to remain alert.

In the midst of no-man's land a mile east of Schwedt the Company came across the first of the bodies. They were Russian infantry. They were lying dead in the dirt; their corpses bloated and swollen from the heat. The air was thick with buzzing flies and the stench of corruption. Raw sewage had attracted rats that scuttled away as the Americans marched by.

Elway led the men through the wasteland. The ground was pockmarked with deep craters filled with stagnant water. The fields were strewn with tangles of barbed wire, discarded equipment and more dead bodies. These were German soldiers, and they had been dead for several days. Elway peered into the drifting grey haze. A few hundred yards ahead he saw ghostly dark silhouettes moving in the grey gloom.

A voice hailed him; the accent unmistakably German. "Are you here to relieve us?"

The men of Bravo Company spread out into a ragged line and went forward, suddenly alert and tense. The silence that hung over the battlefield was eerie and unsettling. The ground underfoot was deeply rutted. One of the Americans stumbled into a ditch filled with three dead German bodies and had to be hauled out of the stinking mire by two of his buddies.

Elway went forward and was met by a Bundeswehr Captain. The German looked aged and haggard. Fatigue had etched deep lines into his face and darkened the rims of his eyes, so they looked sunken in the hollows of their sockets. The German shook Elway's hand and wasted no time beginning his briefing.

"It's been quiet for about twenty minutes," the Bundeswehr Captain told Elway breathlessly. "But the Russians are building up to something, I can feel it. They hit us with artillery and smoke about an hour ago but didn't attack. Intel warned us when we moved up to the front that the enemy had T-72s in this sector, but we haven't seen anything of them. So far it's been wave after wave of massed infantry... but that won't last forever."

Elway looked into the grey distance as though he might see the silhouette of advancing Russian armor, and then, when he saw nothing, he instead turned his attention to the German position. The Bundeswehr Company were dug in along a half-mile of deep trenches. The men standing in the bottom of the long ditch were filthy wretches, only their haunted eyes and teeth showing white through the layers of spattered mud.

"How long have you been holding out here?" Elway frowned.

"Twenty-six hours," the German officer said numbly. "We're out of food, out of water and half my men are wounded or dead."

"Why aren't you with the rest of your Battalion?"

The German pointed to the north. "They're somewhere over there," he said. "We lost radio comms last night when the Russians suddenly launched an attack. We dug in and held our ground and we've been fighting the bastards off ever since."

The battlefront along the German frontier was not the static network of carefully engineered trenches that had criss-crossed the Western Front during the First Great War. Modern warfare was too fluid; too volatile. The battle line between the Allies and the Russians was a blurred fracture of small Company and Battalion-strength conflicts, with individual units welded together through sophisticated communications systems and high-tech weaponry. It meant that in the midst of a concerted enemy attack, whole units could become cut off and isolated from their support network during the rapid cut-and-thrust of a firefight. On the modern battlefield communication was key, and without it, units were vulnerable.

Elway shook his head. "There's no one there," he said gently. "The German units north of here pulled out before dawn. We saw them filing back from the front. You're on your own here. You're the end of the Allied line in this sector."

The German officer gaped as the realization dawned on him. He had no idea he had been fighting off the enemy unsupported, nor that he had been left exposed to the Russians and abandoned by the rest of his Battalion.

"*Verdammter Scheiß!*" the German swore. "For real?"

Elway nodded and made a grim face. "We've been ordered forward to find you. The Army is contracting its lines. We're falling back to the outskirts of Schwedt and establishing a new perimeter."

"*Sohn einer Hündin!*" the Bundeswehr officer swore again, this time with bitter acrimony. He and his men had bled and died to hold a patch of farm field that Allied Command now deemed useless. He felt somehow betrayed. He turned and stared numbly into the smoke haze, and then down at the suffering faces of his men. His shoulders slumped, as if all the fight had been wrenched from him. He nodded his head. "We will move out immediately."

The Germans began filing from the trench, shambling into a rough column. They looked ravaged and haunted by their experience. Suddenly the air overhead filled with a screaming shriek of noise and a hundredth of a second later the ground to the east of the trench line erupted in a savage gout of fire and smoke and whistling shrapnel.

"Take cover!" was all Elway had time to shout before the second artillery round landed nearby. Then the earth began to heave as a salvo of Russian artillery shells erupted around them. The Americans and the Germans flung themselves back into the trenches, cowering for cover as the artillery bombardment rose to a thunderous fury. Elway ducked his head as a round landed short of the trench, heaving clods of earth over his back and collapsing the front lip of the ditch.

Then, through the choking swirls of smoke, Russian infantry appeared.

*

The enemy soldiers emerged to the east of the German trench like ghostly apparitions; vague, ethereal shapes moving with silent menace through the swirling grey smoke. There were still perhaps four hundred yards away, advancing in a loose order skirmish line with their guns on their hips. They were plodding forward like a unit on patrol. Elway narrowed his eyes and tried to estimate the size of the enemy force. He guessed there were at least a Company of enemy troops closing on his position.

A Company he could handle comfortably. What worried him was what the skirmish line of enemy soldiers concealed. Behind them, and still hidden by the smoke, could be the rest of a Battalion, or perhaps Russian armor. He cocked his head to the side and closed his eyes for a second. He thought he could hear the distant rumble and clatter of steel tank tracks, still far away. But the sound was so elusive, shifting on the breeze, that it might well be coming from further to the north or south of their position.

The troops in the trench were a jumble of American and Bundeswehr shoulder to shoulder without organization. Each man had simply scrambled down into the ditch and sought the closest cover. At Elway's side, the German Captain peered over the lip of the dirt ditch and spat.

"These Russians are like vermin," he sneered at the wall of enemy infantry. "They are cockroaches born from street-whore mothers. Killing is too good for them." He snatched up his Heckler & Koch G-36 assault rifle and aimed into the haze.

"Wait!" Elway hissed and seized the German's arm. The Americans had been sent out into the apocalyptic wasteland to retrieve the German Company, not to get slaughtered defending a ditch that the Allies no longer wanted to hold. Elway needed a plan to exfil back to the town, and he needed it quickly. He peered once more into the grey distance and thought he saw the dark shapes of more Russians following those troops that were closing on them.

Elway had fought enough small engagements on the German front to know how the Russians would react to a firefight. The enemy were well equipped, and their troops were well trained – but their commanders lacked any spark of imagination. Time and time again in battle the enemy had repeated the same age-old tactics so that their reactions became predictable. Elway bet his life, and the lives of all the men around him, that the Russians would follow the same routine.

"We're going to open fire on the bastards when I give the word," he assured his German counterpart who was staring into the haze with an expression of vile loathing. "The Russians will fall back if we hit them hard enough and they'll radio for smoke. As soon as the first smoke rounds explode, we retreat towards Schwedt, using their own smoke screen to conceal our withdrawal. When the enemy finally organize themselves to charge, we'll have cleared the area and be within sight of the town's outskirts."

When the Russian infantry line was within three hundred yards of the trench, the Americans and their German allies opened fire. More than thirty enemy soldiers went down in the first few seconds, screaming and bleeding. One Russian soldier clapped his hands to his face and fell moaning with blood spilling between his fingers. The man beside him began to scream in shock, then collapsed, a bullet lodged in his guts. The wasteland of churned dirt turned into a slaughter yard of chaos and confusion. Most of the surviving Russians flung themselves to the ground as a ripple of panic ran through their ranks. Some of the Russians threw down their weapons and fled back into the veil of smoke. Elway knew the first thirty seconds of the firefight were critical. He had the element of surprise and now he must maintain the initiative; that meant pouring a relentless fusillade of fire on the Russians that would prevent them from organizing any kind of concerted resistance.

Heavy machine guns at either end of the trench caught the enemy Company of troops in a wicked crossfire. Smoke hung thick in the air above the trench, stabbed through with the fiery muzzle flashes of the American and German weapons.

"Keep firing!" Elway raised his voice in competition with the savage roar of gunfire.

After the first few seconds, the fusillade became ragged as men along the trench line reloaded. Elway kept his eyes on the smoke-stained ground to the east. The Russians were small hidden lumps in the blood-spattered landscape. Here and there a Russian returned fire but the Americans and Germans were deep down in their trench. A stray bullet fizzed past Elway's face and smacked in the dirt behind him. He ducked down as more bullets plucked at the air above his head. The fire was coming from behind a distant mound of dirt where a handful of Russians armed with a light machine gun were trying to fight back.

"Sergeant Moon!" Elway cupped his hands to his mouth. "There's an enemy machine gun to our right. I want the bastard dead!"

Moon ran crouched along the trench to the nearest heavy machine gun and pointed the target out to the two-man crew. The ground around the enemy position seemed to dissolve into boiling dust as the American gunner hunched behind his weapon and opened fire.

Further along the trench line, the Russians were gradually creeping closer and beginning to fire back in numbers. Elway sensed the tide of the firefight turning. Behind the enemy Company, and still some way in the distance, more dark shadows loomed out of the grey smoke, suggesting there were additional Russian troops organizing themselves to advance and join the battle.

"Hit them hard!" Elway shouted. "Keep pouring fire down on them!"

The Germans – exhausted, low on ammunition and numb with fatigue – fought with contempt for their enemy and with the fanaticism of men possessed. At one point Elway looked up in alarm and saw perhaps thirty of the Bundeswehr preparing to leap from the trench to press home a charge across the muddy wasteland. Only the German Captain's last-second bellowed orders prevented the act of single-minded suicide.

The firefight reached a crescendo and then an eerie lull swept over the battlefield. Elway peered anxiously into the smoke, trying to sense the enemy's next move. Then he heard a salvo of mortar shells arcing through the sky, whistling on the breeze as they descended out of the haze and erupted in thick blooms of white cloud just fifty yards ahead of the trench.

It was the moment Elway had been waiting for; the spreading smoke screen was the precursor to an imminent Russian attack.

"Captain, get your men up and moving back towards Schwedt," Hank Elway knew he had only a few scant seconds to affect their escape. "My men will cover your withdrawal."

"We should stay and fight the scum!" the German Bundeswehr Captain's eyes were still ablaze with defiance. "They defile the Fatherland, the bastards!"

"And if you do stay and fight, you and all your men will die," Elway snapped. His orders were to retrieve the Bundeswehr Company and he intended to carry those orders out. "Now move your ass back to the town!"

The Germans clambered from the trench and began to file west, hidden from the enemy behind the veil of white smoke that had spread upon the battlefield like a heavy blanket. Elway watched the Germans until they became lost in the haze, then turned his attention back to the east. Two more Russian smoke shells burst into thick white blooms thickening the veil but not camouflaging the sounds of infantry moving behind the grey curtain. The impenetrable haze made Elway's flesh crawl and raised the small hairs at the nape of his neck. He knew the Russians were massing to rush the trench, that at any moment enemy troops would come punching through the smoke, firing, and screaming. They would be so close when they appeared that the American troops lining the ditch would be overwhelmed in seconds. But if he withdrew too soon, the Russians might continue to drive towards the town and catch the Germans in the open. If he withdrew too late, he and every one of his men would be slaughtered by the weight of the Russian attack.

He counted down the seconds in his head, his instincts attuned and his ears alert for a sudden clamor of sound that would signal an enemy charge. He waited a full minute, then decided to wait another twenty seconds.

It was long enough. The Germans would be within sight of the town's outskirts. He leaned across to Sergeant Moon and spoke into the man's ear above spurts of sporadic automatic weapons fire.

"Pass the word. We're moving out. I want one last burst of fire and then we high-tail it back to the town."

The Americans opened fire, blazing away blindly into the smoke and then began to fall back towards Schwedt, dropping smoke grenades in their wake to keep the smoke screen about them roiling. Hank Elway was the last man to leave the trench. He stood on the lip of the earthwork for a long moment, emptying the remains of his magazine into the haze and then turned and sprinted to catch up to the rest of the Company.

The Russians still had not attacked and the Americans had completed their rescue mission without a single man wounded.

*

It was late in the afternoon when the column of soldiers finally returned to their rest area seven miles behind the battlefront. There were no transport vehicles to spare and so the Company had been forced to trudge amongst the hellish landscape, past the mounds of dead bodies, over the piles of refuse and rubbish, and through the vile miasma of rotting corruption that hung on the air to reach the relative safety of their bivouac.

Elway's XO was waiting for him with a message. "I don't know if you're in the shit, or you're going to get a medal," Executive Officer Dan Mowbray said. His left arm was in a sling; his body still healing from a bullet wound taken during a firefight with the Russians several days earlier. "But you've been summoned to Battalion Headquarters. The Colonel wants to see you."

Elway frowned. "When?"

"Eighteen hundred," Mowbray looked his Captain up and down. Elway looked like a filth-lathered castaway. "You should just have time for a shit, a shower, and a shave if you hustle."

*

Battalion Headquarters was an abandoned farmhouse seven miles west of Schwedt on the outskirts of a small village named Pinnow. Elway was ushered inside the building by a smartly-uniformed aide and made to wait in a hallway.

After ten minutes of restless agitation, a young Lieutenant beckoned Elway to follow him. They marched down a long cool corridor and stopped in front of a closed door. "The Colonel is ready to see you."

Elway stepped into a disused bedroom that had equipment, boxes and spare radio comms gear piled into each corner. In the middle of the room stood a desk covered with papers and on the far wall hung a large map of eastern Germany.

Lieutenant Colonel Sam Wheatcroft, commanding officer of the 4th Battalion, watched Elway enter the makeshift office from behind his desk. The Colonel took in Elway's drawn face and his deeply sunken eyes but said nothing. There was no room for compassion in war – especially not when every other man in the Battalion was just as tired and just as exhausted.

"How are your troops?"

"Coping, sir," Elway said. "But they could do with some time off the line."

Wheatcroft grunted then glanced guiltily down at his paperwork-littered desk. The look on the senior officer's face left Elway sullen with a sick sense of foreboding. He liked Wheatcroft; he considered the man a good officer, though if Elway could pick a fault, it was with the Colonel's unwillingness to heed advice. Wheatcroft was stubborn as a mule, and just a little too focused on his own promotion prospects for Elway's liking. It meant the Colonel all-too-often volunteered the Battalion for missions they were unprepared for or unsuitable for.

The silence in the room stretched out for long seconds while in the distance a rumble of enemy artillery explosions shook small clouds of dust from the ceiling. Elway peered around the room with red-rimmed eyes until his gaze settled on the wall map. In the past three days, the Allies had been forced to concede ground to the Russians. North and south of Frankfurt an der Oder the battlefront had buckled, almost collapsed completely, and finally been shored up by newly-arrived German troops who had been thrown into the breech to prevent disaster.

"How do you think the fighting is going?" Wheatcroft lifted his eyes, saw Elway studying the map, and forced gruffness into his voice.

Elway sensed underlying nervousness in the Colonel's voice and his frown deepened, the sick slide of unease forming a knot in his guts. "I think we've been getting our ass kicked, sir," Elway opined. "Thank God for the Germans."

"Yes," Wheatcroft conceded grudgingly. "They're good. And there are more Bundeswehr units due to join the line later today. I just heard from Division Headquarters that our Battalion can expect to be relieved by midnight."

Elway arched his brows in unexpected surprise and relief. He started to smile. "That's good news, sir. The men will be pleased to have the chance for some rest. We've been fighting non-stop for the past week."

"Yes…" Wheatcroft's eyes turned shifty again. He found a handful of papers on his desk and read them with exaggerated care, no longer looking at Elway. "Unfortunately, not every Company will be withdrawn to a rest area. Division needs men for an important mission, and I've nominated Bravo Company for the task." For a long moment the words hung in the air. Wheatcroft shifted the papers and snuck Elway a guilty sideways glance. Elway said nothing. He was livid. His lips compressed to a thin pale line and his expression turned accusing. A bitter protest leaped to his lips, but he bit down on the words with a force of will. The Colonel had made his decision and Elway knew there was no way anything he said would change the man's mind.

Encouraged by Elway's silence, the Colonel discarded the paperwork and leaned back in his chair. Now the worst of the meeting was over, he was suddenly mollifying with praise and enthusiasm. "I know your men need a rest, Hank," he used Elway's first name, "but this mission is too important to be left to just any unit. Division wants the best men in theater and I told HQ that there was no one better than you and your troops. It might seem like you're being unfairly overloaded, but in reality, this is an honor. It's recognition of your leadership abilities and the fighting qualities of the soldiers under you."

"Indeed, sir," Elway said woodenly. He didn't need to inhale to smell the bullshit; Wheatcroft was laying it on thick as syrup. "I'll be sure to remind the Company of that when we come under fire."

"I don't expect you will," Wheatcroft said crisply and rose from his chair. He crossed the room and stood before the map. "You're not remaining on the front line. You're heading north on an evac mission."

Elway looked up sharply and caught the Colonel's eye. "An evac?"

"Yes," Wheatcroft described an area on the map with his hand to the north of the battlefront, then paused for a moment as if he were remembering a pre-rehearsed speech. "You're taking your Company to a town named Glauben Sie Stadt. It's about thirty clicks from here. Your mission is to evacuate the local population and to escort an official from the Albanian NATO contingency to safety."

"Sir?" Elway stepped close to the map. Glauben Sie Stadt was about fifteen miles west of the border and well out of the way of any fighting. "I don't understand."

Wheatcroft smiled thinly, then lowered his voice as though what he was about to reveal was confidential. "There's something big brewing," the Colonel began. "Our satellite intel sources have discovered that the Russians are building up their forces to the north of us; they've amassed hundreds of MBTs, and thousands of troops. Allied command fears the Ruskies are about to launch a major attack to outflank us. There are a handful of small towns in the path the Russians are expected to take, and when the attack comes, a lot of German citizens are going to find themselves in harm's way."

"And there's also an Albanian delegate in the area?"

"Yes. He's one of the country's NATO contingency. He's on a 'fact-finding' mission. We need him brought back. Christ knows what would happen if the Russians got their hands on him. It would be a diplomatic and political nightmare."

"Can't German troops handle this?"

"There are Bundeswehr units being deployed to other towns in the region," Wheatcroft assured Elway with a placating gesture of his hands. "Some of the towns closest to the Oder River were evacuated by the Germans several days ago. But we need your troops too. The Germans can't get everywhere in time without help from us."

Elway sighed and nodded. "When do we leave?"

"Dawn tomorrow."

"And how do we get to this town?"

"Oshkosh M-ATVs and trucks are being arranged. And there's one other thing; you have just twenty-four hours to get everyone out of that town and get them to safety."

"One day, sir?"

"Not a minute more," Wheatcroft's expression hardened, and his tone became a sudden dire warning. "Because at dawn the following day we are going to launch the biggest counter-attack of the war. Allied Command knows the Russian attack is imminent, and we have a pretty fair idea of the route they will take and their overall plan. Instead of sitting back and taking another heavy punch, we're going to land one this time. There is a full US Armored Division disembarking as we speak at ports on the German coast; seventeen thousand men and Abrams tanks. Those troops are going to link up with the German 21st Panzer Brigade based at Augustdorf. The

Brigade includes the 203rd Panzer Battalion which comprises forty-four Leopard 2A7 main battle tanks. The Leopards and our Abrams are going to join forces and launch a surprise attack against the Russians. We're going to meet them head on and crush them… and when that happens, Captain, you and your soldiers won't want to be anywhere within twenty miles of ground zero."

Hank Elway nodded. Theoretically, twenty-four hours was ample time to travel thirty miles and load a few hundred people into trucks for evacuation. But Elway had seen enough of war to know that even the simplest tasks were fraught with danger and unseen obstacles. "What about enemy patrols? How close are the nearest Russians?"

"Unknown," Wheatcroft grimaced. "Most likely you will be in and out within a few hours and the operation will proceed smoothly – but it is dangerous country out there," again the Colonel's tone took on the sound of a warning. "So, you go in locked and loaded and you keep your eyes peeled. We don't know when the Russians will launch their attack. If they get wind of what we're planning, they might launch the assault early, or they might have reconnaissance patrols in the area. We have to hope for the best and prepare for the worst."

Elway sighed. "That's very reassuring, sir," he made no attempt to hide his ire.

Chapter 2:

The troops boarded the long line of waiting vehicles while the pre-dawn sky crashed and rumbled to the mindless frenzy of faraway guns.

It had become a gruesome ritual along the German battlefront; the darkness before each new day turned into a cacophony of explosions and slaughter by the massed artillery batteries on both sides of the border. This day the Russian guns were targeting the Allied trenches to the south of Schwedt, and although the Company were several miles to the north, still the dark horizon was lit with the flash and flare of pulsing light as each gun roared and the echo of explosions slammed against the low clouds and made the air tremble.

Hank Elway stood in the darkness beside one of the Oshkosh M-ATVs and watched the winking flares of orange light against the far horizon while around him soldiers clambered aboard their designated vehicles, the men made sullen and surly by their fatigue.

While the troops took up their positions and the guns raged, Elway tried to subdue his fear. The randomness of artillery fire terrified most men; the pure recklessness of fate was something no infantry soldier could ever quite accept. A man could take every reasonable precaution on a battlefield, yet still the risk of death from an errant artillery shell hung over them like an ever-present pall of doom. When the Company had first arrived in Germany, they had marched into a maelstrom of Russian artillery fire that had devastated a section of the Allied line and killed hundreds. The terror of that long ghastly night, crouched in a deep hole while the world around him heaved and erupted and crashed and burned still haunted Elway. It had traumatized the rest of the men in Bravo Company too. Elway saw the unease in Dan Mowbray's expression as the XO approached him out of the darkness. The officer's face was gripped into a tight grimace and his movements were the jerks of a man fighting to retain the outward appearance of composure.

Mowbray approached like he was on a morning stroll, but Elway saw through the thin veil of the façade, though convention and bravado forbade any mention of fear. And so Elway played the game, both men stilted and distracted as they acted out the charade of two composed battle-hardened veterans.

Mowbray glanced over his shoulder and peered back to the south for a long moment. A rent of orange light lit up the breaking dawn and the rumble of the subsequent explosion trembled the earth beneath his boots. Then he cast his eyes overhead. The bellies of the clouds were glowing orange. "Should be a nice day once the cloud thins. I reckon you'll be there and back before chow time," he feigned casual indifference and plucked at the bandages of his wound.

A sudden crack of a Russian shell, sounding much louder than the rest, made Elway flinch. Two days earlier a report spread across the international news services had claimed that the average life-expectancy of a soldier fighting the war in Europe was just forty-one days. Elway was silently figuring the numbers in his head with morbid fatalism. "I hope you're right," he replied, then lifted his own eyes to the skyline. Behind the flashing red fury of the enemy's guns, dawn was breaking, the horizon veiled in grey smoke, so the light came watery and pale across the German countryside. "But when was the last time anything went according to plan?"

"There is that," Mowbray conceded, then lapsed back into awkward silence, looking for something more to say. He turned and watched the Company climbing into the vehicles. "I've put the four rookie replacements that joined us last night into First Platoon. I figured it was the best place for them."

Elway grunted acknowledgement. The Company had lost over twenty men in the past week and there were still precious-few replacements arriving from the States to replenish combat units. Despite all the NATO and US Army assurances, the flow of men into the European theatre was still little more than a trickle. Battalions on the front line were being worn down by the obscene demands of the gods of war, and there was no respite in sight.

The Russian artillery stopped firing suddenly and in the eerie silence of the aftermath the last of the Company boarded the M-ATVs and the vehicle engines roared to life. Diesel exhaust and fumes hung in the air. Mowbray thrust out his hand. "Good luck. I'll see you back here this afternoon. I wish I was going with you."

Elway smiled grimly. "No, you don't," he said. The two men shared a last melancholy moment of foreboding and then Elway turned on his heel, signaling with his arm for the convoy to move out.

The first few miles of the journey took the American vehicles through the outskirts of Schwedt, heading north, past bomb devastated suburbs of charred and crumbled houses, through narrow streets strewn with rubble. A week before, Russian artillery had pounded the town for three relentless days, grinding every building for miles into a mangled pulp of mortar, scorched wood and shattered glass. Elway peered through the passenger-side window of his command vehicle at the scenes of devastation as the vehicles crawled by. The gutters and sidewalks were dotted with the dark crumpled shapes of the dead, the gore and gruesome details of their demise mercifully blanketed by thick drifting smoke, but the stench of rotting flesh was unavoidable. The miasma of fly-blown putrid corruption seeped into the vehicles and coated the back of Elway's throat making him gasp. He had believed himself hardened to the sights and smells of death, but he had never before experienced anything like this.

"Another two miles before we clear the outskirts," the driver was white-faced with his own nausea as he hunched over the Oshkosh's steering wheel, weaving the M-ATV between a slalom course of piled rubble.

As the buildings thinned, the morning light strengthened and the road north beyond the town stretched ahead of them. The fields were gouged with craters of upheaved earth and the roadside lined with the swollen distended bodies of dead cows.

Here and there, Elway caught sight of ruined vehicles; an Abrams tank on its side in a ditch, the carcass of the steel beast streaked with black soot and the hatches thrown open, and nearby, the shattered ruins of a German Marder infantry fighting vehicle. The Marder's front hull was stoved in, and the left side tracks and road wheels had been shattered. On a gentle rise in the distance, marked by a column of black smoke, Elway saw the tailfin of a US F-16 fighter, the rest of the jet's debris scattered across a mile of farm land.

During the first twenty-four hours of the Russian push into Germany, the fields north and south of Schwedt had seen some of the fiercest fighting of the war. Now, a week later, the scars of that earlier battle were still everywhere Hank Elway looked, each one a reminder of his proximity to death.

The four M-ATVs carrying 3rd Platoon were leading the column. Elway's command vehicle and the rest of the Company command element were wedged between the vanguard of the column and the rest of the M-ATVs transporting 1st and 2nd Platoon. Trailing the long line of vehicles was a fleet of six M1083 trucks that would transport the evacuated population of Glauben Sie Stadt south to safety. The M-ATVs were the US Army's newest light utility vehicles, designed to replace the venerable Humvee. A handful of the vehicles in the convoy were fitted with the 12.7mm M2HB turret-mounted heavy machine gun on a ring mount, but the rest carried the M240B. Still, as the unwieldly column finally cleared the outskirts of Schwedt and headed north into open country trailing of a long tail of dust, Elway felt confident the Company had more than enough firepower at its disposal to fend off an unlikely enemy ambush.

As they headed further north, the landscape around them began to change, transitioning from farm lands to gentle rolling hills, the road serpentining through shallow valleys in a series of switch-backs and sudden hairpins. To the left and right of the two-lane blacktop, trees closed in, and they passed through a thatch of woodlands. The vehicles were plunged into sudden shadow; the morning light filtered out by the dense palisade of trees. Then the column began to slow and in irritation Elway snatched for the mic on the vehicle's IAN/PRC-117 multiband radio mounted to the dashboard.

"Six-Three, Six-Six. Why are you stopping, god-damnit?"

"German MPs at a checkpoint," the Lieutenant commanding 3rd Platoon at the head of the column replied to Elway's barked question. "Want me to just blow through and ignore them, sir?"

Elway grimaced. There were checkpoints dotted throughout the German countryside manned by German militia units and Feldjägers. It was a security precaution and a necessity since all of the road signs east of Berlin had been pulled down by German authorities to rob the invading Russians of any basic navigational aids.

"No. I'll be there in a minute."

Elway's vehicle braked to a halt close behind the Oshkosh ahead of it and the rest of the column compressed as it ground to a standstill. Elway climbed down from the M-ATV and went striding forward briskly, his eyes scanning the tree-studded crests of the surrounding hills.

The three Feldjägers at the intersection were polite and efficient. Their ATF Dingo was parked across the road and one of the MPs remained in the vehicle manning the Rheinmetall MG3 machine gun, following protocol. The Feldjägers wanted to know the purpose of the American convoy.

Elway shook hands with the two MPs as they approached him. "We're on our way to Glauben Sie Stadt," he explained. "Orders from Battalion. Is there anything up ahead we should know about?"

"*Nein*, the road is clear," the Germans confirmed, "but the Russians are up to something. Twice yesterday there were reports of enemy contacts northeast of here. There were firefights and men killed, but so far this morning, we have heard nothing on comms."

Elway nodded, his face tight with creeping unease. The Germans reversed the Dingo to clear the road and Elway waved the convoy forward. His command vehicle stopped, and he climbed aboard, gnawing his lip and his brows furrowed. He snatched for the radio again.

"Six-Three, Six-Six. Lieutenant, tell your gunners on those turret-mounted machine guns to stay alert all the way through to Glauben Sie Stadt. We're in hostile territory for the last ten miles of the journey. And tell your driver to step on the gas. We're in a hurry."

Elway issued the same alert order to the rest of the Platoon leaders then sat back in the passenger seat of the M-ATV, peering warily into the distance. Without consciously being aware of it, his hands clenched into tight fists and he sat rigid, like a man bracing himself in the split-second before an imminent collision.

Then it happened.

A column of black boiling smoke appeared from beyond the crest of the hill to his right, followed a moment later by the cracking echo of several explosions, muted by the bellow of the M-ATV's engine, but still distinct and loud inside the vehicle.

What the fuck was that?

"Hit the brakes!" Elway roared, then lunged for the radio. "Explosions and smoke to the north northeast. Stop! Stop! Stop! Everyone weapons ready!"

*

It wasn't much of a town the Russian Colonel decided as he studied the distant mass of buildings from the crest of the hill; just a few dozen homes, a church and a cluster of shops on either side of a single road that ran through the valley before him. But it's location directly in the path of the imminent Russian assault into northern Germany made Glauben Sie Stadt tactically important.

"Send for my Company commanders," the Colonel gruffed, his gaze never leaving the silhouette of the town, scanning each building in turn for any sign of German troops.

"Immediately, sir," the aide lying at the edge of the woods beside the Russian Colonel answered.

Quietly the aide crept back into the dense woods where the Battalion of infantry lay hidden. He found the Company commanders and sent each of them forward to where the Colonel lay in the long grass beneath the fringe of trees.

The day had dawned overcast and smoke-shrouded, the skyline blotted with a black smudge of clouds. But the dull light was more than sufficient to throw the town's profile into silhouette and to give the Russian officer a sense of the challenge he had been set.

The Colonel surveyed the distant buildings one last time and muttered a silent prayer that the German troops defending the town were either asleep in their billets or that they were only Bundeswehr Reservists, posted to secure the location while the German Army's regular Bundeswehr units were fighting on the battlefront further to the south.

One by one the Company commanders appeared in the long grass beside him, slithering forward out of the shadows of the woods until they were at his shoulder.

The Colonel thrust a finger down into the valley. "The road into the town has been barricaded, and has probably been mined as a precaution," the Russian officer said. "I can't see any enemy troops on sentry duty, but we must assume our German friends are not so stupid as to leave the perimeter completely undefended. Therefore, when we attack, we go in hard and fast and brutal, anticipating stiff resistance."

Each Company Captain had their own pair of binoculars. The Colonel lapsed into silence and let the men study the approaches to the town for several minutes while he spoke briefly to his aide. When the Colonel turned his attention back to Glauben Sie Stadt, the steeply-pitched roofs of the distant buildings were being lit by the sunrise. He grunted.

It was time to go to war.

"One Company will launch a frontal assault behind a smoke screen. I want men on either side of the road, and I want them making a lot of noise," the Colonel spoke quietly to his assembled Captains. "They don't have to press home the attack; they just have to keep the bastards interested. A second Company will attack from the north. See that broken section of ridgeline beyond the edge of the trees?"

"Yes, Colonel," one of the Company Captains nodded. He was a grim-faced young man with a shock of dirty blonde hair and a cruel scar across his forehead.

"That's where I want the attack to launch from. Get down the slope as quickly as you can once the distraction begins."

"Yes, Colonel."

"We'll keep the third Company here in the forest in reserve."

The Colonel glanced at his watch and then twisted in the grass to gauge the light. The sun was cresting the hills spilling pale and filtered light down across the valley floor. "We attack in twenty minutes. Get your thumbs out of your asses and get your men organized. Wait for the smoke screen to form, and then go like hell."

*

Behind the broken ridgeline to the north of Glauben Sie Stadt, the Russian Captain and his Company of veterans prepared themselves for action. Some men checked their weapons, others made last-second adjustments to equipment and helmet straps. A Corporal sat with his head bowed over a tattered paperback novel. He looked up suddenly, saw the Company was still not ready to launch their attack, and went back to his reading. Beside him a soldier spat into the grass and then crossed himself. A couple of bottles of vodka were being passed around between the troops to help fortify their courage. The Captain took an indulgent swig, wiped his mouth on the back of his hand, and then made another close inspection of the route down the steep slope of the escarpment through his binoculars.

The Company would have to descend two hundred meters of tree-sprinkled grassy slope to reach the foot of the valley, but from there, the approach to the outskirts of the township was a jumble of rocks, boulders and scraggly undergrowth which would provide good cover – but also slow his men down. On the edge of the town there were several houses and farm buildings surrounded by clumps of trees. Those buildings bothered the Captain. If the farm buildings were defended by the Germans, his men would be ruthlessly slaughtered.

"Sir!" the voice of a Sergeant interrupted the Captain's bleak thoughts and made him swing around urgently.

"What?"

The Sergeant didn't answer. Instead, he simply pointed.

The Captain snatched up his binoculars and trained them on the wooded crest where the Colonel and the remaining two Companies of the Battalion lay concealed. The Captain saw a thin trail of grey smoke rising from within the dense press of trees and a moment later an explosion of thick white cloud burst around the valley floor.

"Tell the men to get ready," the Captain spoke out of the corner of his mouth, his binoculars now trained on the veil of white haze that was spreading like a curtain in front of the town. The Battalion's mortars had opened fire, meaning the diversionary attack was imminent. The Captain watched as a dozen more smoke rounds exploded in quick succession until the entire landscape seemed smudged by a bank of drifting haze.

The sun suddenly burned through the smoke-stained horizon and bathed the township in a moment of glaring bright sunlight. At the same instant a hundred Russian soldiers broke from the cover of the nearby crest and made a frantic dash down the face of the grassy incline, charging towards the road that led to Glauben Sie Stadt.

For long moments the Russians swarmed forward unchallenged. The Captain watched the diversionary attack until the first men reached the banks of white smoke where they were suddenly swallowed up in the haze.

Then a machine gun fired.

From a building on the outskirts of the town, a German light machine gun began shooting up the slope, pouring fire into the smoke screen and the grey shapes that ghosted there. Another German machine gun added its roar to the clamor. The Captain saw the winking flashes of light from distant windows and felt his heartbeat quicken and the palms of his hands turn sweaty. The Russian mortars fired again, thickening the smoke screen. The Captain put down his binoculars and reached for his AK-74.

"Ataka!"

The Russians broke from cover leaped to their feet. The Captain led the charge. His body armor felt like a leaden weight as he scrambled through the long grass, lifting his legs high like he was running through ocean waves. His eyes were fixed on the northern edge of the village. He could hear his men close around him; their harsh breathing, the pounding of their boots and the rattle of their equipment as they tried to keep pace with him. The Captain's initial fears and anxiety gave way to a sense of exhilaration. He understood the urgency of his mission. Every second of delay meant death for the men in the diversionary attack. The other Company were sacrificing themselves to keep the attention of the German defenders fixed to their front, buying him the time he needed to sweep down the slope undetected. But that element of surprise could not stretch forever. Soon an alert German sentry would see the second attack surging from the north and raise the alarm.

The battle clock in the Russian Captain's head began ticking, counting down the seconds. He leaped a cluster of small boulders, landed heavily, and regained his balance. He could hear the long grass swishing about his thighs as he ran on. Sweat broke out on his brow and his breathing became labored. The ground was loose with rocks and crumbling earth as the men swept down the face of the hill in a pell-mell charge.

The Company reached the valley floor and spread out amongst the rocks, loosing cohesion as each man scrambled to find his own path towards the town. The Captain clambered over a boulder and then twisted his head sideways left and right. The Company were swarming forward, grunting and gasping from the immense effort. Then suddenly a man close to him threw his arms in the air and froze, his face wrenched into a rictus of agony. He hung there, seemingly weightless and suspended for a moment, and then tumbled back into the long grass with a stain of bright red blood blooming across his torso. A hundredth of a second later the wicked 'crack' of a rifle whipped against the still morning air.

"Fuck!" the Captain cursed savagely. The Germans were alerted. Now the dash to the town would become a grim and bloody struggle.

A Russian hefting a PKP Pecheneg machine gun threw himself down into the long grass and opened fire, blazing away at a farm building near the town's outskirts.

"Keep going!" the Captain raised his voice and shouted at the men within earshot. "Keep fucking going forward! Go! Go! Go!"

The German fire from the town began as a sporadic sputter of rifles and grew in intensity until the Russians were crawling forward into the face of a roaring avalanche of lead. The Captain threw himself to the ground behind a clump of low rocks and buried his face into the dirt as a flail of bullets cracked and ricocheted over his head. Dramatically a gust of wind stripped the smoke haze away, revealing a clear view to the outskirts of Glauben Sie Stadt. The Captain lifted his eyes and saw he was still two hundred feet from the closest buildings. The Germans were at the windows, picking his men off with ruthless efficiency.

Then a mortar shell, lobbed from a German mortar somewhere within the town, screamed over the Russian Captain's head and exploded in a gout of smoke and lurid red flames. There was a lull of almost a minute while the Germans adjusted their range, then the next mortar plunged down fifty yards to the Captain's left. The exploding shell landed amidst a knot of Russians. One man was heaved into the air, his arms and legs flailing, his body flensed by shrapnel. Two more men went down clutching at wounds and screaming.

Shreds of smoke screen drifted across the battlefront, but it was not enough to shelter the Russians from the lashing whip of the German guns nor the relentless scream of incoming mortar rounds. The grass became spattered with Russian blood. The Captain watched the bloody slaughter of his men with impotent rage and frustration. They were being picked off piecemeal by the Germans and they were pinned down, unable to go forward into that torrent of thrashing fire, and unable to retreat.

They were trapped in no man's land.

The Russian Colonel had watched the attack sweep down the north slope of the crest, first with confidence, and then with a rising sense of bewilderment and frustration as the Germans opened fire and the assault became stalled. Now he prayed he had not hesitated too long.

He rounded on his aide. "Tell the Battalion mortars to fire smoke on the northern edge of the town," he pointed. "And I want those farm houses turned to matchsticks!"

The Russian Captain leading the northern assault on the town was a good officer and an experienced soldier. He had fought in the Baltics and in Poland. The moment the Battalion mortars fired their first smoke shells he leaped bravely to his feet.

"*Ataka!*"

*

The Russians reached the outskirts of Glauben Sie Stadt under a veil of blooming smoke. The men were filled with a savage thirst for revenge. They had suffered terribly from the relentless whip and thrash of the German guns. Now it was time for retribution.

They surged into the town's narrow alleys, screaming their bloodlust. Two German soldiers crouched behind a brick wall opened fire. A Russian Corporal was struck by two bullets and went down in the cobblestoned laneway, dead before his body hit the ground. The men who had been on either side of the Corporal flattened themselves against a stone wall and lobbed grenades. Both Germans were killed in the explosions and the tide of Russians surged on.

A Russian Sergeant leading a handful of men ducked suddenly when a bullet fizzed overhead and smacked against a house wall. The Sergeant peered cautiously around the corner of the building and saw a dozen Germans behind a barricade of overturned furniture and sandbags. The Sergeant looked at the men he had with him. "We're going to charge the bastards," he growled. Now they were in the town, the momentum of the attack had to be maintained. They couldn't allow themselves to be held up by pockets of German resistance, and so the Sergeant would lead his handful of men in a reckless charge, knowing he would probably die in the attack.

He checked his AK-74 had a fresh magazine and then threw himself around the corner, sprinting towards the barricade and firing from the hip as he ran. Around him, screaming their fear and fury, the rest of the Russians followed.

The Germans behind the barricade opened fire.

The Russian Sergeant saw the faces of the enemy through the jumble of their barricade and then everything dissolved into an explosion of smoke and an eruption of hammering gunfire. "Kill the German swine!" the Sergeant ran on through the maelstrom as a frenzy of bullets slashed and cracked around him.

He reached the barricade miraculously uninjured and emptied his magazine into the mass of enemy soldiers from close range. He was swearing with the savagery of a berserker, his face spattered with someone else's blood, his boots sticky with splashed gore. "Die you bastards! Die!" He threw two grenades then ducked down behind a stack of sandbags to reload. The grenades exploded in a violent thunder of noise and fire. Then he was back up on his feet, shooting again; his gun blazing and raging into the tangled bloody mush of the slaughtered Germans until he had no more bullets left to fire.

Throughout the town savage firefights ebbed and flowed as each German position was quickly overrun. Buildings caught fire and the narrow streets became wreathed in smoke. Blood trickled across the cobblestones and spilled into the gutters.

*

The Americans scrambled from their vehicles and Hank Elway led them right, off the road and towards the rise of the nearest slope. He felt his feet reach the incline and suddenly the muscles in his thighs were burning and he had to lean forward into the gradient to keep his balance. He reached for a tuft of grass and clawed his way forward, beginning to ascend the rise of the slope. Elway's first instinct was the get to high ground; the column of vehicles were vulnerable in a ravine surrounded by hills. Once he had elevation, he could scan the horizon to locate the source of the smoke and explosions – and he would have prior warning of an imminent attack on the convoy. He set himself to the steep rise, his lungs starved for air and First Sergeant Joe Moon at his elbow, seemingly handling the slope with irritating ease.

At the crest, Elway threw himself down into the grass and reached for his binoculars. He was breathing like a blown horse, lathered in sweat. He pressed the high-powered lenses to his eyes and swung them towards the north.

The column of smoke was an unmistakable beacon, reaching into the morning sky from two ridge lines away. Elway didn't need a map to know it was the town of Glauben Sie Stadt on fire and burning.

"Fuck!" he swore bitterly and rolled onto his side. The rest of the Company were scattered in the long grass to his left and right. He snarled a long expletive-laden curse and then forced himself to think fast. As the crow flies, he estimated the town was about four clicks north-northeast. On foot, the Company could cover the distance in an hour. It was too long, but he had few other choices. He could hardly charge down the road aboard the M-ATVs with guns blazing – not until he knew the nature of the threat and the strength of the enemy.

"Fuck!" he swore again, then turned to Moon. "Sergeant, detail some men to stay with the vehicles; a driver and a gunner for each M-ATV. They have to be at the ready to attack the town on my orders. The rest of the Company will follow me. We're going to have to hump it on foot the rest of the way to Glauben Sie Stadt."

*

The Russian Colonel stood in the town square and glanced disdainfully at the pile of dead German bodies. The corpses were heaped like cords of firewood, some so bullet-riddled that they were no longer identifiable as human. The Colonel had seen too much horror and devastation to be disturbed by the sight. In war, death was inevitable.

"Casualties?" he asked his Operations officer.

"We lost thirty-two men, and another fifteen are seriously wounded," the officer replied crisply. "Our injured are being moved to the hotel where they can be attended to."

"The German wounded?"

"They have been dealt with in the usual manner, sir," which, the Colonel knew, meant the enemy's injured soldiers had been executed.

"Citizenry?"

"We have captured one hundred and fourteen Germans who were residents in the town. The majority are women. We have also captured a middle-aged man who claims he is a diplomat attached to the Albanian NATO contingency. He was found hiding under a bed in the hotel. With him was a naked young woman who he claims she is his personal assistant." The Operations officer handed over the man's seized passport, and a handful of documents. "He had these in a briefcase."

The Russian Colonel's eyes arched with sudden interest. He flicked through the pages of the seized passport and his expression turned cunning with unexpected triumph. "Where is this man? Have you interviewed him or the girl?"

"Not yet, sir."

"Do so – quickly. They might have information about the enemy. After you have finished your interrogation, I will want to speak to them personally. See to it."

"Immediately, Colonel." The officer was about to turn on his heel and stride away when the senior officer had a sudden after thought.

"Where is the Captain who led the attack?" The assault down into the valley from the northern slope had been well executed under difficult conditions, and the Colonel wanted to recognize the man who had led the charge for his bravery.

"The Captain is dead, sir," the Operations officer said. "His body is being retrieved as we speak. He died on the outskirts of the town."

The Colonel lapsed into a moment of silence. It was not an expression of grief or remorse, or even solemn respect. He was simply trying to recall the name of a man who could replace the dead officer. "Very well. Have Lieutenant Sokolov report to me once the town's perimeter has been secured."

The Colonel and his Operations officer walked through the outskirts of Glauben Sie Stadt until they reached the far edge of the town where the road meandered on through the saddle of the valley. To the north and to the west, the terrain was lush and green and undisturbed. It seemed like another world...

But not for much longer, the Colonel thought with a grim smile. Once the Russians launched their offensive against the northern flank of the Allied lines, Berlin would fall, and the Russians would sweep further west and then north towards the German coast. His mission was a key part of that strategy, paving the way for the looming attack. So far, everything was going according to plan.

The Colonel turned to his Operations officer and smirked smug satisfaction. "Get a message to High Command. Tell them that Glauben Sie Stadt has been secured. The path west into the heart of Germany is wide open and awaiting our tanks."

Chapter 3:

The American Company went forward quickly, trekking cross-country and guided by the pall of smoke from the burning town. When they reached the valley floor before the final ridge that separated them from Glauben Sie Stadt, Elway paused to gather his Command element around him.

"First and Second Platoon," he pointed uphill, "I want you halfway up the rise, in that dead ground," he indicated a gentle grassy ridge. "The mortars will set up here and I want the two HMGs and FIST (the Fire Support Team) with me and Third Platoon."

The first two Platoons began to ascend the slope. Sergeant Moon nudged Elway's elbow. "The explosions have stopped," he noted with his head turned and his ear cocked. "Sounds like we're too late to the party."

"Maybe," Elway said sourly. God alone knew what he would find when he reached the top of the crest and peered into the valley beyond.

Once the first two Platoons were in position halfway up the slope, Elway waved the rest of the Company forward. They went up the grassy rise easily, continuing past the first two platoons towards the crest. The summit of the ridge was crowned with a jumble of weather-worn rocks. Elway waved 3rd Platoon down into cover, then crawled ahead to the skyline… and saw Russian soldiers.

"Damn it!" Elway muttered under his breath as he peered down into the narrow streets of Glauben Sie Stadt.

The town was on fire.

The Russian infantry were going from building to building, looting and searching for townsfolk who had attempted to hide themselves from the attackers. A hugely muscled soldier appeared on the sidewalk of a narrow laneway dragging a screaming woman by the arm. The woman was howling in fear, her face white with her terror. She was pleading with the Russian for mercy, sobbing through an unintelligible stream of German. Elway didn't need to speak the language in order to understand. The front of the woman's dress had been torn open and there was blood on her knees. Elway watched the tiny vignette of drama unfold through his binoculars, sickened by the horror in the woman's voice.

The Russian dragged the woman towards the town's square. She slipped suddenly and fell to the cobblestones. Another Russian soldier dashed from the shadows and threw himself on top of her, baying like a wild animal. The woman tried to fight the man off, pummeling him with her fists and thrashing her legs until the soldier drove his elbow into her face. She went suddenly limp. Two more Russian soldiers helped carry the woman behind the wall of a house. She screamed once more, the sound a pitiful, plaintive wail, and then fell silent.

"Fucking scum," Joe Moon breathed, his face twisted with his revulsion. He had crawled to the crest to join Elway.

"She's not the only woman they found, judging by the screams," Elway said bitterly.

He put the binoculars down and scanned the township with impotent rage. He guessed there were as many as three hundred Russians marauding through the streets, pillaging and burning; probably a combat Battalion of infantry, though he could see no evidence of IFV or tank support. Still, three hundred men was a force far too powerful for Elway's Company to do battle with.

"What are we going to do?" Sergeant Moon stared down into the mayhem with vile loathing. He saw the pile of bullet-riddled bodies that had been stacked in the center of the town. "Do we try a frontal attack before they can secure the perimeter and set up machine gun posts?"

Elway turned his head, frowning. "There will be no attack," he said, hating his helplessness.

"But Captain!" Moon looked appalled. "We have orders to evacuate the townsfolk."

Elway's eyes hardened. "Look, I'd love nothing more than to charge down the hill, guns blazing and kill every one of those Russian fuckers," his voice trembled. "But there's no place for emotion in combat, Sergeant. Despite the atrocities the enemy troops are committing, the fact is that they outnumber us by three-to-one. The only logical solution is to contact Battalion HQ, let them know that the Russians have beaten us to Glauben Sie Stadt, and await fresh orders or reinforcements."

"There won't be a soul left alive to evacuate by the time Battalion makes a decision," the words came from Moon's mouth cold and bitter.

"Better a hundred dead German townsfolk than a hundred dead US Army infantry," Elway said callously.

Sergeant Moon slid back down the slope in silent disgust and Elway could feel the man's contempt. Behind his back he heard disgruntled muttering coming from some of the nearby soldiers, but he ignored the discontent, for he was just as outraged as the rest of his men. He feared his conviction for caution would crack if anyone dared voice a challenge. And so he stayed at the crest alone for several more minutes, sick in the guts with helplessness as he watched German women and children being hunted down like rats while all around them the smoke thickened as the township continued to burn.

Then, suddenly, a thunder of automatic weapons fire slammed and echoed against the sullen smoke-stained sky.

*

"What the fuck was that?"

Elway looked up sharply and his eyes scanned the ridgeline on the opposite side of the valley. The slope was sprinkled with trees and shadowed by a wooded grove due north of where the Americans were hidden. Joe Moon crawled back up to the skyline, his face set and his eyes everywhere at once. "It sounded like a light machine gun," he had heard the wicked whip-crack of gunfire, the echo of the sound slightly muted by distance.

Then the far skyline seemed to sprout a hundred or more dark shapes; men moving purposefully down the hill, wading through the long grass with weapons raised. Elway snatched up the binoculars and felt himself tense.

"They're German Bundeswehr!" he gaped. "At least Company strength."

As Elway and Moon watched on, the German infantry swept down the slope and then took cover in the rocks to the north of the town. Two heartbeats later a fusillade of machine gun fire from the far ridge punched holes in the wall of a building on the town's outskirts. It was the signal the German infantry had been waiting for. Behind a savage roar, they rose to their feet and dashed from the rocks towards the township, crossing the broken ground with their weapons at their hips.

The Russians in Glauben Sie Stadt were slow to respond to the imminent danger. A handful of enemy infantry opened fire on the approaching Bundeswehr. Two Germans went down in the long grass, folding forward at the knees. The Germans returned fire and the machine guns overwatching the attack from the far ridge added their own throaty roar to the crackling fusillade. Then more Russians appeared, moving in small groups through the town towards the sounds of fighting, shouting in confusion and alarm as the drifting smoke from burning buildings wafted around them.

The Germans moved swiftly across the boulder-strewn ground, but the Russians were well-organized. After the initial shock of a surprise attack, the enemy marshalled their forces to the north of the town and the German assault began to stall in the face of a wall of sizzling lead. Elway watched the firefight through his binoculars and saw a handful of Germans launch a sudden rush for a farm building. They never made it. Russians appeared from the shadows at the end of a narrow lane and opened fire on the heroic Bundeswehr, killing them all in three savage blazing seconds of gunfire. Then the ground ahead of the German troops amongst the rocks heaved around a blinding flash and a billow of smoke.

"The Russians must have mortars somewhere in the town," Elway muttered, though he was too absorbed in watching the firefight to search the surrounding streets for the Russian weapons. The German attack had been bold and impulsive. For the first few seconds the element of surprise had carried the Bundeswehr to the valley floor, but now their rashness was being punished. The attack had bogged down and become a pitched battle. It was inevitable that the Germans would now suffer.

"We can't let them just die for no reason," Joe Moon pleaded.

Elway gnawed his lip. "A hundred Germans and our Company?" he said dubiously. The sums didn't add up in the American's favor.

"The last thing the Russians will expect is another surprise attack from the south," Moon pushed his case for the Company to join the fight. "And we're no longer talking about civilians. We're talking about our Allies in this war. We owe them, sir," he added the honorific as an afterthought, aware that he had already overstepped his authority.

Another Russian mortar round exploded amidst the German positions, and in the violent flash of light and flung dirt Elway saw a soldier's body picked up and spun cartwheeling through the air.

Hank Elway made his decision.

"Get the Platoon leaders together," Elway ordered Moon. "And get on the radio to the M-ATVs. I want them here in two minutes. Tell them we are launching an attack on the town against a Battalion of Russian infantry. They're to come in hard and fast with all guns blazing."

When Moon returned to the crest, he had the Company's Platoon leaders with him. Elway spoke quickly. "I want the two HMGs set up here on the skyline to cover our attack and I want the mortars to fire smoke on that town. As soon as the first smoke round strikes, we go down the slope. 1st Platoon will secure the town square. 2nd and 3rd Platoon will push to the northern edge of the town and attack the Russian defenders from the rear. Get your men ready. We move out in exactly one minute."

Now the decision had been made and he was committed to carrying the attack through, Elway chaffed at the sixty second delay until the mortars lobbed their first rounds. He didn't want to deal with the doubts and remorse that he knew would surely follow his decision – yet he needed the smoke cover. And so he sat, with his heart thumping against the cage of his ribs, and he distracted himself with thoughts of his wife and kids back home in Arkansas until he heard the familiar and distinctive cough of the Company's two 60mm mortars. Two seconds later the valley floor began to fill with a veil of drifting white smoke.

"Attack!" Elway scrambled to his feet, relieved that the time for tortured regrets was finally over. All that mattered now was action. On his order the line of men either side of him rose from out of the grass.

"Attack!"

*

The American infantry swarmed over the rise and advanced in a ragged line down the steep face of the grassy slope. Elway had his eyes fixed on the nearest buildings, expecting at any moment to hear startled exclamations from the Russians and then the first scatter of gunfire, but the only sound was the harsh rasp of his breathing and the heavy thump of his pounding steps. He ran through a skein of white drifting smoke then felt the murky haze surround him as he reached the valley floor and sprinted towards the nearest buildings. The mortars were still firing but their sound was muffled by the shattering fury of the firefight along the northern outskirts.

A dark shape loomed out of the smoke and Elway realized it was a building. He slowed in his run, slammed his shoulder against the building's stone wall and took a moment to catch his breath. Men emerged from the smoke as grey drifting shapes, coming forward at a run, moving to the left and right as the attack became an urban battlefield.

Somewhere nearby an automatic weapon fired, but Elway could not tell whether it was an M4 or a Russian AK-74, so similar were the sounds of both weapons. He stepped out from the cover of the wall and found himself at the end of a narrow street lined with small houses on either side. A Russian appeared in one of the doorways to Elway's right. The soldier was bare-chested. He was huge beast of a man with scruffy beard stubble and a shaved head. He had his weapon in his right hand and a bewildered, irritated expression on his face. He saw Elway and opened his mouth to scream a warning. Elway shouldered his M4 and fired instinctively. The bullet caught the Russian soldier in the middle of the chest and sent him staggering backwards. The Russian flailed his arms for a handhold that wasn't there and fell into the shadows of the doorway. Elway sprang forward, cautious but needing to close the range quickly before the enemy soldier could recover his weapon. Just as Elway reached the sidewalk the Russian appeared in the doorframe. His chest was splashed with blood, and his movements were like a drunkard. He threw up his weapon and swayed as he fired. Bullets fizzed and cracked about Elway's face, missing him by inches. Elway fired again on the run. His first two shots smacked into the front wall of the house but the third caught the Russian in the shoulder. The AK-74 slipped from his hands and his eyes grew wide. Elway shot the Russian in the head from close range and ran through the door into the darkened gloom of the little house. He could hear weeping from a back room.

"Americans!" he shouted as he stumbled down a shadow-struck hallway. The closest door was open. Elway swung around and flung himself across the threshold. There was a blonde-haired woman sitting on the bed. She had her knees up to her chin, her arms hugging her naked body. She was swaying slowly, her eyes vacant with trauma. "Americans!" Elway took in the entire scene in an instant. "Are you alone? Are there any other Russians in the house?"

The woman shook her head. Elway spun on his heel. A roar of automatic weapons fire sounded raggedly from one of the houses further along the street. Elway burst out through the front door and back into the smoke-filtered daylight. "Second and Third Platoon, make for the northern edge of the town! Move it, soldiers!"

Elway ran on, following the sounds of gunfire. It was impossible to command a Company of men in an urban battlefield; the fighting became too fragmented for cohesion and so the men must simply fight and trust their extensive training to give them the advantage. Elway fought like just another infantryman, moving north, using the buildings ahead of him as cover, his eyes moving and his head constantly turning as the firefight seemed to swell in intensity. A handful of men from Third Platoon appeared at an intersection ahead of him. Elway dashed across the blacktop to join them.

The men on the sidewalk were blood-spattered with cuts, but still in the fight. One of the men was the Company RTO, weighed down by a backpack radio. Elway spent sixty seconds huddled in the doorway of a bullet-riddled café on comms to his Platoon leaders. "Westland, give me a SITREP!" the Lieutenant leading First Platoon had not responded to Elway's initial comms call. When he tried a second time, Elway's patience had run out. "Westland! Are you fucking alive?"

Lieutenant Paul Westland finally replied. His voice was thick and wavering with static. In the background Elway could hear sporadic gunfire and the *'crump!'* of a grenade exploding.

"We're in the town square!" Westland reported. "Taking heavy fire from buildings to our east. The fucking Ruskies just blew the fuck out of a house I had four men in with a fucking RPG!"

"Casualties?"

"I've got four men dead and three injured."

"Fuck!" Elway grimaced. "What's the strength of the enemy?"

"I dunno. Maybe a dozen. They're holed up in a house and some kind of a town hall."

Elway thought fast. As he stood there a bullet smacked into the doorframe of the café, missing his head by a few inches.

He flinched and ducked instinctively. The men around him returned fire on a house further down the street. Elway dropped to his knee to make himself a smaller target while the fury of the sudden firefight erupted all around him. "Get on comms to the M-ATVs. Tell them to head to the town square when they enter the town. Fucking direct them over the radio if you have to. Hit those fuckers in the building with one of the 50cals if necessary but clean them out. Understand?"

"Roger that," Westland said, then his voice was drowned out by a nearby roar of machine gun fire. Elway threw down the radio mic and turned all his attention onto his own predicament. There was at least one shooter in a building about two hundred yards down the road. Bullets whipped and cracked off the sidewalk and the men knotted around the Captain had scant little cover. Elway knew it was just a matter of time before they took hits if they didn't move – now.

"Follow me!" he shouted.

The handful of Americans scattered from their positions like an offensive team breaking from a huddle. As they ran towards the gunfire, Elway pointed left at a low stone wall. Two men peeled off and made for the fence, trying to encircle the house where the enemy were barricaded. Elway and the rest ran on, moving in short fits and starts between the hard cover of doorways, sidewalk trash bins and service alleys between the buildings. Suddenly Elway saw the silhouetted head and shoulders of an enemy soldier in an upstairs window of the target building. The man fired and the soldier at Elway's shoulder went down.

"Chips!" Elway saw the woman fall from out of the corner of his eye and doubled back. Sergeant Elaine 'Chips' Fry was down on one knee, her face wrenched into a rictus of agony and a bullet lodged in her right thigh. Elway hooked his arms under the woman's shoulders and dragged her through the bullet-splintered door of a house, trailing a thick smear of the Sergeant's blood behind him.

Fry was white-faced with shock, her skin waxen and her eyes brimming with tears. She had a blood-trickling cut across her brow that was a superficial wound, but it was bleeding profusely, streaking her face in a red running mask. Elway clamped his hand over the woman's thigh wound and fumbled for an IFAK (Individual First Aid Kit).

"Are you good to go?" Elway shoved his face close and shouted.

Fry's eyes seemed to regain focus like a person jolted awake. Her gaze swam for a second then fixed. "Yeah," she said, then louder, "Fuck yeah!"

Elway handed her a spare mag. "Cover us," he staunched the woman's wound with a haemostatic dressing. "Hooah?"

"Hooah!"

Elway snatched up his M4 and went back out through the door into the street. The rest of his group were returning fire on the window, blazing away to suppress the enemy soldier. As best Elway could tell, it was a single shooter. He sprinted forward, making a mad dash for a doorway fifty yards ahead of him. The Russian in the house leaped brazenly to his feet and fired down into the street, emptying an entire magazine and missing with every shot. Elway reached the door lightheaded and dripping sweat. He ducked into cover.

The front of the house the Russian was firing from was just two buildings away. Elway tried to toss a grenade through the gunman's window, but the grenade missed and exploded harmlessly on the street. He reached for a smoke grenade but before he threw it there was a sudden explosion on the far side of the target house and then a brief, savage exchange of gunfire. Ten seconds later the two men Elway had sent over the stone wall to encircle the building appeared framed in the shattered upstairs window. One of the men gave a 'thumbs-up' signal and shouted, "All clear. Fucker is minced meat."

There were three enemy soldiers in the house, two of them dead on the ground floor and the shooter dead in the upstairs bedroom. Elway stalked through the house quickly. One of the dead Russians on the ground floor was slumped with his back against the splintered wood of an overturned table. Elway barely gave the bodies a second glance. He swarmed up the stairs and found a north-facing room. From the window he had a view through steeply-pitched rooftops to the outskirts of the town. The buildings there were wreathed in veils of smoke, stabbed through with red flaring muzzle flashes – evidence that the Germans still fought heroically and that the Russians had still not been overwhelmed.

"Move your asses!" Elway came down the stairs. "The fight ain't over yet."

The small knot of soldiers moved on while ahead of them assault rifles and light machine guns continued to bark. Elway caught sight of four men hugging a wall and firing into the distance. "Where's your Lieutenant?" Elway snapped.

One of the men pointed towards a maze of narrow service alleys that ran behind a block of houses. Elway went forward and found 2nd Platoon crouched in cover behind a long brick wall. The Lieutenant leading the Platoon was sitting hunched with his back against the wall, one hand pressed to his ear and the other clutching a comms mic. The man looked up, startled to see Captain Elway standing over him.

"SITREP!" Elway demanded.

"We're pinned down by RPGs and LMG fire," the Lieutenant summed up the tactical situation in a handful of words. "There's some kind of school or office block two hundred yards to our front."

"Casualties?"

"Six wounded."

"Enemy?"

The Lieutenant shrugged. "Can't say. At least a squad, maybe a Platoon."

Elway grunted. The attack was stalling. He didn't know where 3rd Platoon were, but he sensed the firefight to the north was beginning to peter out. "Give me your radio."

The Platoon RTO connected Elway to the lead M-ATV in the approaching convoy. Elway kept his message succinct. "Hobbs, move your fucking ass! We are pinned down and the attack is stalling. We've got German allies under heavy fire and Russians between us and where we need to be, so move your fucking ass and get here asap!"

"We're inbound now!" Sergeant Hobbs' voice was loud with his own urgency. "ETA twenty seconds. Where do you want us?"

Elway answered intuitively. "Send the 50cals to the town square. Just tell them to follow the main road through the heart of the town. I want the rest of the M-ATVs to head to the northern edge of the town. We'll rendezvous with them. The Russians are holding several buildings on the outskirts and there are Germans north of the town, so watch what you fire at."

Elway cut comms and looked around. "Where are your Javelin teams?"

The Lieutenant pointed. The two-man teams were hunkered down at the far end of the wall.

"What about your AT4s?"

The AT4 was a Swedish-designed 84mm unguided, single-shot, disposable recoilless anti-tank weapon. The American Army's M136 AT4 version of the weapon carried modified launch tube bumpers, sights and slings. Each combat squad was allocated at least one of the weapons.

The Lieutenant pointed at the riflemen bearing the AT4s, then ducked and flinched as the brick wall they were sheltering behind suddenly heaved and blew apart from an explosion. Shards of shattered masonry flew like shrapnel as the wall and the Americans sheltering in its lee were consumed in a smoking fireball. For a moment the world seemed eerily still, and then the screaming began. Elway picked himself up off the rubble-strewn ground. His ears were ringing, and his vision was blurred. He put a hand to his forehead, and it came away sticky with fresh blood. He scraped the muck from his eyes and stared dazedly around him. Half a dozen men were down, writhing in the dust and debris. One soldier's face was a mask of pulped raw flesh and blood, his jaw hanging slack and his eye sockets empty. He screamed and screamed in terror and agony. "I'm fuckin' blind! Oh, God! I'm fucking blind!" Two medics staggered through the smoke and pinned the man down to pump him full of morphine, then smothered his ravaged, shredded face with field dressings because there was nothing else they could do. Another man lay curled up in the fetal position, clutching his guts. He was sobbing softly, calling for his mother. His legs kicked in convulsive spasms. One of his buddies rolled the man onto his back and then retched explosively when he saw the man's guts had been flensed from his body and now lay in a purple ropy mess in his lap.

Elway felt himself sway on his feet. The black roiling cloud of smoke stung his eyes and caught in the back of his throat. He gagged, spat a mouthful of dust and grit, then scraped the back of his hand across his mouth. A twenty-foot-long hole had been gouged out of the brick wall. Through the gaping rent he could see the enemy-held building in the near distance. It looked to Elway like a two-story block of apartments. He grabbed one of the riflemen with an AT4 slung over his shoulder and pointed.

"Fire at the fucking building!" he shouted, his ears still ringing so the sounds of the firefight blazing all around him seemed dull and muted. A spray of automatic weapons fire plucked and zinged off the ruined brick wall, but Elway didn't even flinch. "Bring the whole fucking building down!"

The AT4 was remarkably simple to use, especially against a target as huge as a building. The rifleman unslung the weapon and dropped to one knee, then removed the safety pin at the rear of the tube, unblocking the firing rod. He tugged on the front and rear sight covers and the weapon's iron sights popped up into their firing position.

"Fire in the hole!" Elway called to warn the other soldiers. The back blast of an AT4 could cause severe burns and overpressure injuries to anyone unfortunate enough to be caught unawares. While troops scattered the rifleman removed the weapon's first safety and took aim on the ground-floor doors of the building.

"We follow the shot!" Elway lifted his voice and screamed the order. "As soon as the projectile hits, we charge the fuckers!"

The man operating the AT4 pressed the red firing button with his right thumb and the projectile streaked across the urban wasteland and exploded in a huge fireball of flames and brewing smoke. The explosion seemed massive – out of all proportion to a typical AT4 hit, and for an instant Elway wondered if maybe the building's gas pipes had been ruptured and detonated by the strike.

"Follow me!" he screamed, and clambered through the rubble.

The rest of the Platoon forced themselves to their feet and ran bravely through the smoke, jinking and weaving between outcrops of small cover, fear in their faces, anticipating the meaty sock of a bullet that would kill them. Elway had the same fear; it welled up like a lump in his chest and constricted his breathing so that every lumbering step was punctuated by a ragged gasp for air. He pushed himself on, eyes burning as he peered into the smoke scrims, looking for danger. The façade of the building had been ripped away by the explosion and the western wall teetered on the verge of collapse. Elway threw a grenade into the ruins and saw the limp figure of a Russian soldier laying under a pile of shattered masonry. Elway put a bullet in the man's head and ran on.

When he reached the ruined building, the rest of the Platoon were around him. Several shots rang out. Two more dazed, bleeding Russian soldiers were shot before they could throw up a weapon to fire, or throw up their hands to surrender. The Americans cleared the building with ruthless professionalism.

In the heart-thumping aftermath, Elway caught sight of the first M-ATVs. Three of the vehicles were barreling down a laneway, coming on quickly. He stepped out into their path and waved them towards the scatter of buildings still to the north of where he stood. He figured the last of the Russians had contracted to a block of houses and were now sandwiched between the Germans and his men.

Elway and the remnants of 2nd Platoon followed the M-ATVs. The vehicles took up hull-down positions in the ruins of several small houses and opened fire on the last row of buildings. Elway could hear the Russians still fighting on, their attention directed towards the Germans amongst the rocks who had been unable to advance and were now coming under heavy fire.

Two riflemen bearing AT4s fired their projectiles at a house on the corner of the Russian-occupied block and then a Javelin team launched a projectile at a house to their left. "Go! Go! Go!" Elway slapped the back of the Lieutenant leading 2nd Platoon and the men ran forward, slipping and stumbling through debris and smoke. Elway ran to the nearest M-ATV and directed the gunner to pour his fire onto the upper-floor windows of a building. "Suppress them!" he barked.

The battlefield erupted into sixty long seconds of violent machine gun fire and grenade explosions and then stopped abruptly. When the smoke cleared, Elway saw a ragged line of grey bedraggled and bleeding shapes shuffling towards him.

The surviving Russians had surrendered.

Chapter 4:

He was about the same age as Elway; a man with short dark hair, pale skin and a strong jaw. He held his head with a hint of haughty Teutonic arrogance as he introduced himself.

"I am *Hauptmann* Kurt Wolf, commander of A Company, 371st Panzergrenadier Battalion," the German introduced himself in accented English.

Elway thrust out his hand. "Good to meet you, Captain," Elway had a genuine respect for the German soldiers. They were tough, well-trained and disciplined. "Hank Elway, Bravo Company, 4th Battalion."

The two men silently sized each other up. Elway had a cut above his brow, patched with a field dressing that hung over his right eye. His uniform was smoke and dust-stained and spattered with someone else's blood. His face was sweaty with grime, but the German officer looked equally haggard. His face was grazed and there were dark shadows of fatigue and exhaustion below his eyes.

"We saw your attack," Elway said. "If you don't mind me saying, I thought it was a bold risk to take, given that you were heavily outnumbered."

The German arched his eyes and his expression changed. Elway's delicately chosen words, both men knew, were a thinly veiled rebuke for an impulsive assault that could have easily ended in disaster.

"You watched our attack?" the German Captain's voice turned accusing.

"Yes. From the southern ridge of the valley."

"So you were in position, you witnessed the murder, rape and execution of innocent German women and children... and yet you did nothing until after my own attack had already engaged the Russians?"

Elway flinched. The German's scolding sounded like an accusation of cowardice. "Fools rush in where sensible men fear to tread," Elway distorted the expression. "We were calling for support from Battalion."

The German Captain bridled. "I wonder, Captain Elway, whether you would have been so cautious if America was being invaded and it was your own women and children being brutally slaughtered. You accuse me of recklessness, but how could any man stand by and watch his kin murdered in cold blood and not take action, regardless of the dangers and risks?"

Hank Elway said nothing.

For another long moment the two Captains bristled with antagonism until a sudden shout from the far side of the town square broke the tension.

The German Company had suffered heavy casualties during the firefight. The American medics were working tirelessly to tend to the wounded alongside their German equivalents. The injured were laid out in ragged lines on the blood-slick cobblestones. From a doorway on the far side of the square two American soldiers from 1st Platoon appeared, escorting a middle-aged man and a young blonde woman. Elway narrowed his eyes. The girl looked obscenely young; her tender body still not fully formed. The shouting man who was sandwiched between the two soldiers flung his arms in the air as he approached, stepping over and through the ranks of injured warriors as if they were an irritating obstacle.

"Who fucking runs charge here?" the man blustered in badly mangled and heavily accented English. He was elegantly dressed in an Italian suit and had an aura of self-importance and distinction in the way he carried himself. "Who is big boss of fucking soldiers?"

Elway and Wolf exchanged glances, neither of them wanting the additional problem the man represented.

"I am," Elway sacrificed himself. "Captain Hank Elway, US Army."

"Do you know who I am, Captain?"

"Yes sir, you're an Albanian delegate to your country's NATO contingent and you've been in Glauben Sie Stadt on a fact-finding mission with your 'assistant'," Elway flicked a glance at the girl standing in the man's shadow. She was winsomely beautiful with enormous blue eyes and a thin waif-like figure. She was dressed in a T-shirt and jeans.

The Albanian delegate nodded his head. "I am very important man. You must get me safely to Schwedt."

"That's one of the reasons we're here, sir," Elway said. "So, if you'll just be patient while we load the civilian survivors and our wounded first, we'll make room for you in one of the trucks waiting just down the road a ways."

"A truck?" the Albanian looked mortified. "You have not brought a car – a BMW?"

Elway kept his expression impassive but let some of his irritation sharpen his words. "No. This is a combat zone and we're a combat unit. We're not here to chauffer you, we're here to haul your ass back to safety before the entire Russian Army comes surging west."

The Albanian bridled but saw the implacable expression on Elway's face. He gave Elway a last withering look and retreated to the far side of the courtyard with his arm around the girl, clutching at the shreds of his dignity.

"So, you know too?" Captain Wolf spoke again only after the Albanian official was out of earshot.

"Know what?"

"You know about the imminent Russian drive into western Germany designed to encircle the Allied flank."

"Yes. We were sent to evacuate the townsfolk and escort them to safety. The Russians got here before us."

Wolf nodded. "Then we find ourselves on similar missions," he smiled thinly; an expression without humor. "My Company has been sent to search for Russian electronic warfare systems. If there is an attack coming, the Russians will position sophisticated EWS units to disrupt Allied communications and satellites. We're hunting the bastards."

"What are you looking for?"

"Krasukhas," the German officer revealed.

The Krasukha-2 was a highly mobile and very powerful electronic warfare system the Russians had mounted onto an 8x8 Baz truck. It was designed to jam drones, AWACS, recce aircraft and satellites in order to disrupt comms and command networks. It could also play havoc with the fire-control radars aboard fighter jets. The Russians normally deployed the Krasukha-2 to defend their Iskander missile batteries and often paired a Krasukha 2 with the model 4 variant which was designed to disrupt low-orbit satellites and ground based radars from hundreds of miles away. The system rendered satellites useless. Together, the two units could completely disrupt an Allied counter-attack or rapid response efforts to the Russian incursion.

Elway grunted but said nothing. Medics began carrying the most seriously wounded soldiers to the M-ATVs. As soon as each vehicle was loaded, it sped from the town square, heading back to Schwedt.

"They're mobile units," the German Captain went on. "It's like trying to find someone's needles in a stack of hay, yes?"

Elway was only half-listening to the German's problem. He had more immediate concerns. It was entirely possible that more Russian troops were in the vicinity and were, even at that moment, speeding towards Glauben Sier Stadt.

"Well, I wish you every success," Elway shook the German's hand civilly and then turned on his heel and began barking orders.

A few minutes later the fleet of six M1083 trucks arrived in the town and the loading of surviving civilians for evacuation to safety began.

*

The fleet of M-ATVs and trucks drove towards the smoke-veiled south. The entire distant horizon lay under a pall of black billowing haze. Elway spent most of the journey on the radio, making a SITREP to Battalion HQ and detailing the firefight with the Russians. When the convoy finally reached the outskirts of Schwedt, the evidence of fresh enemy artillery destruction was everywhere they looked. Houses were on fire and two apartment blocks that had been standing at dawn were now gutted shells, their roofs collapsed and flames leaping high into the afternoon sky. There were dead bodies on the sidewalk and a fleet of Army M997A2 Humvee Ambulances blocking one lane of the road into town, waiting to carry the mutilated corpses away.

Colonel Wheatcroft was beside the main road, sitting in the passenger seat of a HQ Humvee. Humvees were being used by command elements because there still were not enough of the newer M-ATVs in theatre for the combat troops.

The column ground to a halt while the medics tended to the dead and dying on the roadside. Elway climbed down from his vehicle and went towards the Colonel's Humvee, moving like an old man, his body stiff and sore in places he could never have imagined.

Wheatcroft sat with a map of eastern German across his knees. He was staring at it with a frown of concentration as Elway approached, then looked up abruptly at the last moment, for an instant his eyes blank. Slowly recognition came into the Colonel's eyes, and he stared fixedly at Elway.

"You look like you've been through hell, Elway."

"Yes, sir," Hank Elway said, and fingered the gauze bandage above his eye. "I've got eight men dead and a handful wounded."

"Damn," the Colonel grimaced. His expression was harried from an accumulation of bad news. Elway's casualty report was just another immense weight that must be added to the burden of command. The Allied troops were stretched wafer thin and in the air was the intangible sense that at any moment the entire line might fracture and collapse. A fusillade of Russian artillery arced high overhead, whistling through the smoke scrims. The rounds landed about a mile west of where the two men stood and struck buildings on the town's outskirts. More smoke and fire bloomed, dragged south by a nagging breeze that filled the air with soot and embers.

"We're in trouble," the Colonel glanced obliquely at Elway as though wishing to avoid direct eye contact. "The German troops meant to relieve the Battalion on the front lines were attacked by Russian Su-25 ground attack aircraft about ten miles west of here an hour ago. The Germans were shot up pretty bad; over fifty percent casualties and a handful of convoy vehicles destroyed before our fighters could respond and intercept."

"So, there's no relief coming, sir?" Elway latched onto the one piece of news that mattered to him most and his voice was heavy with despair.

"I'm afraid not. 4th Battalion has been ordered to hold the line and remain at the battlefront until more reserves can be found – or until our armored counter-attack can strike the enemy. Your men have an hour to chow down before they move forward again. You'll be covering Sector 6-1; it's to the north east of the town."

"Fuck!" the disappointment spilled from Elway is a single expletive. He wasn't sure how much more the men of Bravo Company could take. The relentless fighting, danger and fear had worn every soldier down to the point of exhaustion.

A look of annoyance flashed across the Colonel's tight features and he bridled, "It's not just Bravo Company, dammit. The entire Battalion will be in the trenches."

"Sir, my troops are –" dutifully Elway made a half-hearted attempt to plead his case for time at a rest area.

"I don't want to hear it, Captain!" Wheatcroft snapped. "This isn't a question of choice, it's a matter of necessity. Shit rolls downhill. Regiment hands down the orders to Battalion and I pass the orders on to you – now do your god-damned job."

An ambulance roared past, jouncing and swaying over rubble and around craters to speed its cargo of injured and maimed to a field hospital. Elway watched the vehicle race by, his shoulders slumped and bitter frustration working his mouth into a thin pale line of resentment.

"Yes, sir," Elway said woodenly, then turned with a flare of temper. "Will you be visiting the front lines, sir – to get a sense of the enemy's strength? Bravo Company would certainly be happy to show you what front line combat is all about."

It was a spiteful barb, dripping with provocation. The Colonel's face flushed deeply, and Elway enjoyed a moment of silent triumph. Then the Colonel's expression re-composed itself; his features hardened and the movements of his hands as he folded the map became fussy and precise. "I know what it's like at the battlefront, Captain," the Colonel snapped, "And if you ever speak to me like that again, I'll relieve you of command and bring you up on charges."

Elway did not reply for a long moment, but in the aftermath of the exchange he regretted his moment of malice. He knew Wheatcroft was only doing his job, and he knew too that every other Allied unit fighting along the battlefront was under the same intense pressure. Combat command came with a heavy millstone of responsibility and the higher the rank, the heavier the burden. Wheatcroft was caught between a rock and a hard place – giving orders he didn't want to give to men who had fought themselves to the point of collapse. The only glue that held such a mechanism in place was the men's training and the iron chain-links of rigid military discipline. The bristling antagonism between Elway and Wheatcroft was an indication of just how finely strained the Allied Army was becoming under the relentless pressure of the Russian advance.

In the absence of a response, Colonel Wheatcroft, turned and glared his Captain, his eyes swinging like the loaded barrels of a shotgun. "Are we clear, Captain Elway?"

"Yes, sir," Elway said indignantly and trudged back to the waiting column of M-ATVs.

*

The road through Schwedt that led east to the frontlines was choked with the gruesome tide of war; the cratered blacktop filled with troops trudging in both directions, the flow of bodies blurring until the scene became a thrall of drab mud-spattered swaying motion.

Headed west, away from the fighting, staggered the survivors of the battle, their bodies broken and bleeding, their faces gaunt and their eyes haunted from the horror they had endured. The uninjured helped carry the mutilated, bearing them on stretchers or dragging them slumped over their shoulders while ambulances nudged their way through the milling sea of despair, forcing the men to the rutted verges of the road, diesel fumes adding to the putrid stench of death and sweat and fear that hung in the air like a cloying mist.

There were more dead by the roadside where the men were forced to march, some of the bodies part-buried in the mud, others, their flesh rotting and their corpses bloated, were swarming with flies.

Against that tide of human misery and towards the roaring guns marched the 4th Battalion, the men of Bravo Company in the lead, while ahead in the distance the sky flamed and flickered red with fury.

The Company marched in two lines, humping their equipment and heavy weapons, their eyes down, their bodies racked with mind-numbing fatigue. They went towards the fighting with shuffling grim-faced lethargy, each of them lost in their own thoughts and seemingly numb to the proximity of danger, as if life had ceased to matter.

At the head of the column, Hank Elway peered through the smoke haze until he could make out the distant low ridge that marked the battlefront. The ground was chewed by artillery fire, pockmarked by craters, and appeared as a vast ugly scar that had been scraped across the fertile farm fields. Nothing seemed to move in the distant smoke. Black tortured tree stumps stood like twisted ghosts in the haze and a dark ragged line ran through the heart of the muddy ruin, indicating the Allied trenches.

Elway felt his despair wash over him. Sector 6-1 was at the northern end of the Allied line; a mile-long section of shallow trench that had been hacked out of the muddy ground and was being defended by a Company of French infantry. The trench was cruelly exposed to Russian artillery fire. Even as he looked on, enemy rounds crashed in the distance, heaving up great gouts of dirt and debris and smudging the ridge with a veil of sinister grey smoke.

Elway led his troops off the road and through a muddy rutted field. As they marched closer to the ridge, the obscene stench of death seemed to thicken. The soldiers' steps began to shorten, and the progress of the column slowed as if with sudden tremulous reluctance. Sergeant Moon barked angrily.

"Keep going! Move it!" he sniped at the ranks.

The Company reached the foot of the ridge and Elway followed the rise of the slope with his eyes. It was a gentle incline of not more than fifty feet, but in that moment it appeared as daunting as Everest. Between him and the trench was a ravaged muddy litter of shattered equipment, eviscerated bodies, flames and roiling smoke. The dead lay like discarded detritus, their corpses mangled, some partly submerged in the mud. Elway wove a ragged course up the incline, his boots slipping in the ankle-deep mire and the breath forced from him in explosive grunts. The column of Americans filed past a destroyed French Army VBMR Griffon, the armored vehicle overturned in the mud and the left side of the APC torn wide open by a Russian artillery round. There were bodies in the carnage, but Elway did not stop to stare. Instead he marched stolidly on until, through the smoke, the lip of a trench appeared and he saw the helmeted heads of the French soldiers.

A voice called out a challenge in French and although Elway did not know the language, he replied. "We're Americans," he said. "Bravo Company, 4th Battalion, 6th Infantry regiment. We've been ordered to relieve you."

A man's face emerged through the smoke. He was standing in a dugout, his head lifted. His face was smeared with mud, his features barely recognizable. Only his haunted eyes showed white. "I am *chef de bataillon* Lavigne," the man offered Elway a weary wave. The rank was equivalent to a Major in the US Army.

"Captain Hank Elway," the American replied. Saluting was forbidden in combat situations because the gesture might alert enemy snipers to the proximity of a high-ranking officer, so instead Elway dropped down to his haunches on the lip of the trench until the two men were almost eye-to-eye. "My men are here to relieve you, sir," Elway put some compassion into his voice. The French infantry looked like forlorn bloodied urchins.

"Thank God," the French officer nodded. "Get your men in cover, Captain. The Russians are due to hit us again any moment. I'll lead you forward."

Bravo Company climbed down into the communications trench and the French Major led the file of men forward. They reached a T-intersection where the communication trench connected with the frontline trench and Elway looked about him in barely-concealed horror.

The French soldiers defending the ridge were standing knee deep in sloshing mud, their bodies so thickly coated in the mire that they appeared like shapeless blobs in the haze. The front lip of the trench had been reinforced with sandbags but here and there a Russian artillery round had collapsed the earthwork. In two places at either end of the French line, the men had dug deep holes into the trench's forward wall where they stored food rations and spare ammunition. A pile of dead bodies marked the end of the French position, the mud-covered corpses stiff with the onset of rigor-mortis and crawling with scavenging rats.

It was hell on earth.

And then the gates of perdition opened.

Russian artillery fired on the ridge, drowning the Americans and French in a sudden deluge of flames and heaving earth. It was a thunderous fury unlike anything Elway or his men had previously experienced. The French and Americans cowered helplessly in the muddy trench for thirty cataclysmic minutes while the Russian guns turned the air around them into a furnace of shrapnel-filled horror.

When the storm was over, the men emerged from the maelstrom bleary eyed and dazed, their ears ringing and their senses reeling. They peered into the haze white-faced and shaken. Two Americans were down in the sloshing mud, both of them hit with shrapnel. One woman was clutching at her shoulder and grimacing through the waves of pain as they washed over her. The other man lay face-down, his body limp and unmoving.

The remnants of the French Company withdrew through the communications trench, carrying their wounded and abandoning their dead because there were simply too many bodies to be moved without the aid of vehicles. The Americans took their places along the front wall of the trench. Elway positioned the HMGs at either end of the line and ordered the Company mortars, FIST and RTOs back to the relative safety of the communications trench.

"We're as ready as we'll ever be," Sergeant Moon said when the men were in place. Not even the sucking muddy mire seemed to discourage the man as he moved back and forth along the line, chivvying each soldier to alertness.

The Russians attacked just an hour later.

In previous wars fought from trenches, military doctrine and the near proximity of the enemy's lines had led to a philosophy of overwhelming firepower from close range. But in the fields of eastern Germany, the Allies had abandoned the theory and instead opted for a policy of 'getting your licks in early'. Partially this was because advances in weaponry had led to accurate firepower at greater ranges, and partially from the notion that it was best to jab repeatedly at the enemy rather than let them get close enough to overwhelm a defended position. When the first Russian BMP-2s appeared in the distance, two thousand yards away and made hazy by dense smoke, Elway did not hesitate.

"Alert the Javelin teams," he ordered Sergeant Moon. "Take those fuckers out before they cross the valley floor."

Each of the dozen mud-streaked BMP-2s in sight would be loaded with a handful men, Elway figured, and following in their wake would be more infantry, advancing in the shelter of their steel bulk. It added up to a Battalion-sized enemy attack, against his under-strength Company.

The FGM-148 Javelin was an American man-portable fire-and-forget anti-tank missile that used an infrared guidance system. The Javelin's HEAT warheads were capable of defeating even the most modern Russian tanks.

The Javelins fired. Their missiles launched from the CLUs and streaked skyward on thin tails of grey smoke. Elway lost sight of the first missile in the drifting smoke-drenched haze but six seconds later one of the enemy armored personnel carriers suddenly exploded in a fireball of flames.

The explosion was puny compared to the thunder of an artillery round and was muted by distance. The explosion appeared as a flash of red light on the far horizon that flared for just a few seconds then disappeared behind a smudge of black smoke. Elway snarled with savage triumph. "Hit the bastards again – and keep hitting them until you run out of reloads."

There was no thought of carefully husbanding the Javelin reloads; saving a few of the lethal missiles until the enemy were at close range. The Javelin was most effective at longer distances where the missile could plunge down out of the sky and strike the enemy vehicle's thin top armor.

The Javelin teams fired again and scored more hits. The Russian BMP-2s accelerated and began to weave and jounce across the crater-strewn ground. They were hampered by the mud, their steel tracks throwing up huge sprays of churned earth as they surged forward to close the range and bring their turret-mounted 30mm autocannons to bear. The infantry following the armored personnel carriers were suddenly stranded and exposed across the valley floor. They came on in a broken ragged line, wading through the glutinous mud but moving slowly. When they were within a thousand yards, the Company's M240B/L machine guns added their roar to the battlefield. Sixty seconds later Bravo Company's 60mm mortars joined the fray.

The Russian attack began to fracture and lose cohesion, their plight exacerbated by the unforgiving terrain. The BMP-2s could not slow to offer the infantry cover, and the infantry could not advance quickly enough to keep pace with their supporting armor. The assault broke into two distinct waves and allowed Elway the chance to deal with the threat piecemeal rather than face the brunt of a combined assault.

The Russian machine guns mounted atop the surviving IFVs opened fire, bullets socking into the front wall of sandbags protecting the American position. Elway ducked and waded through the knee-high mud searching for his FIST. The Lieutenant commanding the Company Fire Support Team was squatting in the mud of the communications trench, hunched over his comms equipment. Elway snapped his instructions in a single long exhalation of breath. "I want arty to drop everything they've got on the valley to our east. Tell them to bring the heat asap!"

It wasn't that simple. Calling in fire support required a strict radio procedure, ranging information and co-ordinates. The Lieutenant put his head down and went to frantic work.

When Elway returned to the frontline trench, two more Russian BMP-2s were on fire. One of the vehicles was stalled in the mud; its sides sooted black and the carcass of the vehicle still smoldering. The remains of the second BMP lay scattered across a hundred yards of open field, the vehicle's guts ripped out and flung in every direction by the awesome impact of a Javelin missile. There were bodies in the mud, one of them on fire, and the others laying in crumpled heaps.

The machine guns at either end of the trench cut a withering swathe through the Russian infantry's ranks. The Americans had the high ground and the Russians made easy targets. Even before they closed within effective range of the troops bearing M4s, Elway sensed the enemy attack was already faltering.

A mortar round landed fifty yards short of the Russian infantry, but rather than adjust their range, the mortar team simply continued to fire – daring the Russians to advance through the storm of explosions and whistling shrapnel. The soldiers that did run the gauntlet were mercilessly cut down; the slaughter concealed behind a bank of low-hanging smoke.

The first Allied artillery round signaled the end of the Russian attack. The 155mm HE round plunged down from out of the sky and fell a hundred yards beyond the enemy infantry – but the roar of the explosion and the sudden new threat was enough to stall the enemy infantry's advance and send it scattering back towards the far horizon. Hounded by more Allied artillery explosions the Russian APCs retreated, just four of the dozen BMP-2s left intact by the time they reached the far skyline and were blanketed from sight by the smoke.

The Russians attacked again thirty minutes later. This time the enemy infantry poured forward, pressing the Allied positions further to the south. Elway and the troops of Bravo Company stood and watched the firefight from their trench as three Battalions of Russian soldiers supported by more BMP-2s drove forward. The ground between the Oder River and the outskirts of Schwedt was low-lying marshland and delta, intercut with swamp-like stagnant water that made it difficult for the infantry to advance. The bridges across the Oder and the bridge on the eastern outskirts of the town had long ago been destroyed, so now the Russian troops were forced to traverse the marshy ground across a series of narrow portable pontoons.

The BMP-2s had no such troubles. The amphibious armored fighting vehicles waded through the swampy ground in a great roaring swarm of diesel engines and autocannon fire.

Allied artillery south of the town was quick to respond to the concerted attack. Within minutes the first artillery shells began to rain down on the Russians, causing chaos amongst the attackers and fracturing the momentum of their advance. The infantry, caught in the swamp-like mire, broke into smaller ragged groups but still pushed forward. The BMP-2s reached the very outskirts of Schwedt and ran headlong into a wall of American, German, and French anti-tank missile fire.

Elway watched the battle unfold through his binoculars as the smoke shroud around the town thickened and the echo of each new artillery salvo slammed against the sky. He could see the plight of the enemy's infantry, and as a soldier, he felt a pang of professional remorse. The ground underfoot made it impossible for the enemy troops to advance in good order and in the absence of a covering smoke screen, they were dying in droves. For several futile minutes the Russian soldiers tried vainly to keep pace with the surging wall of BMP-2s and then a sudden storm of Allied artillery fire put a brutal end to their advance. Several of the pontoon bridges spanning the marshes were destroyed and the infantry found themselves stranded. They began to fall back towards the Oder. Elway focused his binoculars on one of the steel bridges and saw a knot of enemy infantry trying to push forward into a storm of light arms fire while all around them the boggy ground heaved and ruptured from artillery hits. There was an officer amidst the Russian troops, waving his arm and urging his men forward. Then suddenly two US AH-64 Apache helicopters appeared to turn the tide of the fight.

The Apaches dropped down out of the veil of smoke overhead, ugly menacing monsters of the battlefield, with their M230 chain guns roaring. The Russians on the pontoon bridge were stranded. They were slaughtered to a man in just a few savage seconds. The American helicopters swooped north, their guns still roaring and then climbed back up into the cloud cover, chased from the battlefield by Russian SAMs launched from a Pantsir-S1 on the Polish side of the border. The Apaches flew directly over Bravo Company as they sought to evade the Russian missiles, the pilots in the helicopters flinging their aircraft about the sky, pumping the air full of chaff, and activating their onboard electronic countermeasures in a desperate bid to avoid being struck. One of the Apaches flew on westward, lost in the smoke, but the other was hit by one of the Russian SAMs and destroyed in mid-air. The explosion bloomed overhead like a gruesome fireworks display and seconds later smoking twisted debris began to rain down across the battlefield.

The last of the BMP-2s reached the outskirts of Schwedt and disgorged the mechanized troops they had been carrying. The Russian soldiers spilled out through the rear door hatches of each vehicle into a wicked crossfire of Allied machine guns concealed amongst the town's rubble. The BMPs returned covering fire, their autocannons flailing, but the Russian infantry were caught in a firestorm and savagely mauled.

The first of the BMPs began to fall back. Without infantry support they could not push forward into the town itself. The surviving Russian infantry went with the vehicles, still fighting bravely, but retreating. The firefight south of the town intensified and then ebbed. Elway could judge the momentum of the battle by the percussive sound of the explosions and the flurries of small arms fire. He no longer needed the binoculars to know the Russian attack had failed. Over the next few minutes, the sound of gunfire slowly petered out and the snarl of smoke around the eastern fringe of the town gradually began to diffuse.

Elway exhaled with relief. Overhead the day was darkening towards dusk and the Russians had so far avoided night attacks during the German campaign. Instead, the enemy's guns opened fire again, a prelude to a long terrible night that would follow.

The first week of the German campaign had gone favorably for the Russians. The Allies had committed themselves to a static line of defense along the border and by doing so had played inadvertently to Russia's strengths. Since Soviet times, the Russians had built a military doctrine around using its ground forces to pin an enemy to a position in order to then decimate them with massed artillery. In Germany, with the Allies clinging to their trenches, the troops on the frontline became prime targets for the Russian guns and there was little a soldier could do other than cower in the bottom of his hole and pray for fate's kindness to survive.

When the first Russian guns opened fire and the skyline to the east began to flicker with the eerie red glow of the approaching storm, Elway ordered the survivors of Bravo Company deep into the mud-filled trench. Overhead the air fizzed and cracked with explosions and a hail of shrapnel. The ground around them heaved and the air turned heated and thick with dust. Elway pressed his shoulder against the front wall of the trench and could feel the quake-like ground tremors as each round exploded. Within a matter of minutes he was numb and deafened, his senses swimming like a boxer at the end of fifteen rounds. At Sergeant Moon's suggestion, the Company had humped extra rations and cans of soda into battle. Now Elway ordered the food and drinks distributed. It did nothing to lessen the dreadful impact of each exploding enemy round, but at least, for a short while, the men were distracted by something other than their nightmarish terror.

*

The Russian barrage continued well into the night and when the last enemy gun fell silent the Americans emerged from the filth and mud and were forced to stand on high alert for an hour, prepared for a possible Russian ground assault. The men were tired to the point of exhaustion, their nerves frayed, and their senses numbed. They stood with their weapons at the ready until Elway was sure an attack was not coming.

Then, from behind the trench line and from the direction of Schwedt, they heard an engine, grinding up and down through the gears until it stopped abruptly. Fifteen minutes later Colonel Wheatcroft appeared out of the darkness, kitted out in full combat gear and carrying an M4.

Wheatcroft slid down into the stinking mire, feigned casual indifference to the fetid stench and the cloying mud, and went along the trench line in search of Elway. The Captain was standing post at the northern end of the trench beside one of the Company's M240B/L machine guns. When he saw the

Colonel's face loom out of the eerie darkness, Elway recoiled in shock.

"Colonel?"

"I thought I'd take you up on your invitation to visit the battlefront, Elway," Wheatcroft said. "In fact, I thought you and some of your Bravo boys might like to accompany the old man on a patrol. Division wants a grove of woods four clicks to the north of us scouted tonight. The Allied counter-attack is due to reach us by mid-morning tomorrow and the General doesn't want any unforeseen enemy surprises that can be avoided."

It wasn't quite an order, but nor was it a question. Elway shrugged his shoulders. "How many men, sir?"

"Your best Platoon. We need to travel light and fast. We'll take a couple of AT4s but nothing else other than personal weapons and water. We've only got until daylight before all hell is going to break loose and the biggest tank battle of the war erupts all around us."

Elway left the Lieutenant leading 2nd Platoon in command and chose 3rd Platoon for the patrol. Perversely, the men in the Platoon seemed enthusiastic about the mission; glad that, for at least the next few hours, they would be free from the stinking mud and away from the lethal menace of Russian artillery.

They moved out before midnight, the men carrying just their M4s, and two of the riflemen bearing recoilless anti-tank weapons slung over their shoulders. They followed the spine of the ridge and then went down the slope and into the distance in single file with the Colonel leading the way.

"What do we do if we encounter an enemy force, sir?" Elway asked.

"We're a recce patrol," Wheatcroft reminded him. "If we encounter anything suspicious, we radio HQ and call in the arty."

Once on level ground, the men moved quickly through the shadow-struck night. They moved in single file, well-spaced, their eyes searching the darkness for the first signs of danger. Sergeant Moon trailed the column, nudging the men ahead of him with the butt of his weapon and a harshly whispered word if their step slowed.

The ground was farmland that folded into small dips and rises, woven through by a beaten earth track that meandered a lazy course ahead of them. Elway suspected it was a cattle-trail used by local farmers to move cows from one paddock to the other for the grass was flattened and worn beneath their feet, though he was sure the cows were long dead.

As they marched, Elway's mind turned to the task ahead. He doubted a Platoon patrol would find anything of note. A major Russian troop build-up in the vicinity would have been spotted by Allied satellites, and anything less than Company strength was hardly a threat to the mass of German Leopards, Abrams tanks and thousands of Allied infantry converging on this patch of Germany. Yet despite the apparent futility of the exercise, he too was as grateful as the rest of the men to be free from the muddy trench line for a few hours.

An hour after they set out, the Platoon came within sight of the woods. It appeared as a darker dense mass against the night sky, its silhouette hazed by skeins of drifting smoke. The men rested in a small fold of ground while Elway and the Colonel made their plans.

"We'll circle around to the west, then approach the woods from our side of the lines," the Colonel decided because it was the best way to avoid a blue-on-blue tragedy. He had been assured by Division that there would be no other Allied patrols in the area, but still he chose the most cautious option.

Elway nodded. "And if we encounter an enemy force, sir?"

"We assess," the Colonel reiterated his earlier instructions. Elway detected some rising tension in Wheatcroft's voice. "We're not looking for a fight if we can avoid it. We're searching for signs of enemy activity that might be a threat to the counter-attack. Our first option is to report to HQ and let the arty handle it."

Chapter 5:

When the Platoon reached the edge of the woods, Elway and the Colonel paused one final time, listening. The night seemed alive with the small sounds of nature and, overlaying them, the constant muted rumble of far-away artillery fire.

Wheatcroft glanced at his wristwatch and pressed his lips together with small annoyance. It had taken longer than he had expected to reach the woods. "Two hours," he told Elway. "We cover as much ground as we can in that time."

They went forward in single file with Elway leading the column, the Colonel in the middle of the line and Sergeant Moon trailing. Once they were through the dense outer perimeter of trees, the forest thinned, and the trees grew more sparsely. Elway went as quickly as caution would allow, guided by the images he was seeing through his ENVG-B goggles.

Each man wore the Army's new Enhanced Night Vision Goggle-Binoculars that had been designed to provide US soldiers with sharper night vision images than previous generation models. The new goggles employed white phosphor tubes that made the green-glow of earlier model goggles obsolete. As well as lighting up enemy targets with a white halo, the goggles also provided a wider view to increase situational awareness and the ability to see through layers of smoke. As Elway pushed forward, trees and terrain features loomed out of the blackness, making the column's progress steady and surefooted.

They moved deeper into the forest, and the ground around them began to change. The trees grew just as thickly, but the undergrowth and carpet of leaves gave way to drifts of thigh-high grass. The level ground began to contour and fold, following the remnants of a dry watercourse east towards the Oder.

They reached the foreslope of a gentle rise of forested ground and peered ahead from their elevated position. Elway frowned, uncertain. He thought he caught a whiff of diesel exhaust, and then dismissed the notion. Instead, he waited until the rest of the Platoon caught up and then glanced at Colonel Wheatcroft questioningly.

"Continue east?" Elway asked quietly. He was sure there were no Russians within miles, and yet he felt compelled to whisper the question. Wheatcroft joined him at the crest of the gentle slope and peered ahead. The reverse side of the slope lead down to an area of broken rocky ground. He shifted his gaze north but saw little in the darkness.

"Yes," Wheatcroft decided. "Continue east..." He was about to say more when Elway caught the Colonel's arm and urged him to silence, then cocked his head to the side.

He stayed in that position for several seconds until finally the sound that had alerted him separated itself from the background ambience of the forested night. The small noises of nature faded and in its place was a faint indistinct 'clank' of metal against metal. Elway and Wheatcroft exchanged urgent glances and the men's attitudes became suddenly guarded. They shouldered their weapons and began moving quickly towards cover. Elway compelled them to stillness with an urgent hand gesture.

The sound came again a few seconds later, carried on the fitful breeze. Elway turned like a hunting dog, his ears attuned to the night, trying to pinpoint its direction.

"East northeast," he ventured, then pointed.

The Platoon moved out again, scrambling down the reverse slope of the rise, keen for the cover of the dark trees below them. Elway stood to the side of the line as it snaked forward through the undergrowth, making sure no man was lagging. When Joe Moon reached him, he put his head close to the Sergeant's and whispered fresh instructions.

"Take the lead for a while," he ordered Moon. "Keep heading east northeast."

The Sergeant nodded. No other acknowledgement was needed. He went forward at a jog and Elway waited for a count of ten before he set out after the column, putting twenty yards between himself and the trailing man should the Platoon suddenly be encircled and ambushed from the rear.

The Platoon continued to descend into a shallow wooded valley and then came to a trickling stream. They waded through the ankle-deep water and then set themselves to the next rise. The dry riverbank was littered with rocks and the men were forced to sling their weapons and use their hands to clamber back up to level ground.

Suddenly the wall of trees ahead of Joe Moon separated and through a gap in the blackly silhouetted palisade the Sergeant saw straight angular shapes; slab-sided rectangles and a blur of erratic movement glowing bright white through his goggles.

Without turning, he froze on the spot and the breath slammed in his chest. He raised his fist level with his head to order *'Freeze!'*, then lifted his carbine to the ready position at shoulder level and pointed the weapon directly ahead to signal, *'Enemy in Sight'*. The Platoon went rigid and began to sink to the ground, the air suddenly crackling with tension. Moon made a final silent signal, pointing to the rim of his helmet. It was the sign for Elway to move to the front of the column.

It all happened in absolute silence. Elway ghosted forward, crouching low and doubled-over. With him went Colonel Wheatcroft. The rest of the Platoon dropped prone to the long grassy ground and took up firing positions, moving like wraiths in the dark.

With Elway close beside him Joe Moon pointed ahead into the night.

Elway could feel rivulets of cold sweat trickle from beneath the rim of his helmet and run down his unshaven cheek. For a long moment he saw nothing but the outline of a dense wall of trees and foliage glowing white. He tilted his head, shuffling to the right a few feet, then swore.

"Fuck!" Elway croaked in hoarse shock.

Through the wall of trees emerged the shapes of four enemy IFVs and a long eight-wheeled truck bordered in glowing neon light. Moving around the vehicles were several dozen men; more than Elway could count.

He continued to peer into the night, barely daring to breath. Beside him he felt Colonel Wheatcroft tug gently at his sleeve. Elway turned his head slowly to conceal his movement and got eye-to-eye with the Colonel. Wheatcroft inclined his head, gesturing back in the direction of the dry riverbed. Elway nodded once slowly.

The Americans retreated to the riverbank, slithering on their bellies like snakes. One by one they dropped down out of sight and crouched in the ankle-deep water.

Elway was breathing heavily, adrenaline fizzing in his veins. He ordered two men to remain stationed at the lip of the shallow gorge as lookouts, then squatted down with his face just inches from the Colonel's.

"Did you see them, sir – through the gap in the trees?"

"Yes," Wheatcroft was already planning a route out of the woods. "Four IFVs – probably BMP-2s – and maybe a full Company of soldiers."

"And the truck, sir. Did you see the eight-wheeler?"

Wheatcroft shrugged. "Sure. So what?"

"So, it's a Russian Krasukha, sir!"

"Are you sure?" Wheatcroft's tone betrayed his dubious disbelief.

Elway nodded vehemently. "The Germans we fought alongside at Glauben Sie Stadt were detailed to search the area for a mobile Krasukha 2 and a Krasukha 4. I talked to the German officer after the Russians surrendered. He told me that High Command was concerned those two advanced EWS systems could disrupt comms for the approaching Allied armored attack and interfere with our satellites, so they detailed the German Company to search for the units and destroy them," Elway thought fast. He wished now that he had paid more attention to the German Captain. He racked his brain for additional details. "They're also a key component of any planned Russian attack. Finding one of those units this far into Germany proves the Russians are building up to an attack of their own."

Wheatcroft grimaced. He knew perfectly well the significance of the Russian EWS vehicle, though its discovery in the woods presented a serious problem. He shot Elway a sideways glance. "Okay," he nodded, keeping his voice to a whisper. "We'll double time it back to the edge of the woods. As soon as we are well clear of the Russians, we'll radio HQ and call in an air strike."

Elway shook his head. "Take another look, sir," he insisted. "The Russians are clearing the area. They're preparing to move. The Krasukha is a mobile unit. If we wait until we're clear of the woods to call in an air strike, the damned thing could be miles from here by the time the fly-boys drop their bombs. We have to take it out – while we have the chance."

"Are you crazy?" Wheatcroft snapped and his face in the darkness reflected his sharp horror. "We can't take on four IFVs and Christ-knows how many armed Russians. There could be a full Company of enemy soldiers and each of those BMPs has an autocannon. We'll last thirty seconds."

"I know," Elway admitted grimly. Launching an attack against such overwhelming numbers and against such massive firepower was suicidal. "But we ain't got a choice."

Wheatcroft leaned closer to Elway so his voice was a confidential husk that no other man in the Platoon could overhear. "I'm not here to get killed, Captain. I'm here on a recce mission. We've done our duty – we found evidence that the Russians have a Krasukha mobile EWS system in the vicinity. My orders from Division are clear. We exfil the area and we call on comms for fresh orders."

"Colonel, if we walk out of these woods without first destroying that enemy EWS system, hundreds, if not thousands of Allied lives will be put at risk. Their presence in Germany could jeopardize the entire Allied attack."

Wheatcroft made a bitter face and glanced at his watch, his features running with sweat, and his entire body tight with tension. In less than eight hours' time a full Division of American soldiers and a combined force of over a hundred Abrams and Leopard tanks were due to crash against the

Russian flank. By midday the woods where Wheatcroft and 3rd Platoon were now hidden would probably have been shredded with HE rounds and littered with hundreds of dead bodies – as would much of the terrain for miles around them.

In the path of the Allied advance was a Russian force preparing its own imminent attack... and the Krasukhas, which had the ability to determine the outcome of the conflict.

"You said the Germans you met at Glauben Sie Stadt were hunting two of these systems?" Wheatcroft snapped, not liking his options.

"Yes," Elway nodded.

"Has the other one been destroyed?"

"The Germans were still hunting them when I spoke to their officer this morning."

"Then if we take this one out, and kill ourselves in the process, it still does not negate the threat the second system poses. We could die here and achieve nothing."

Elway nodded. "Sir, I don't know how the Russian Krasukhas work. I don't know if the two systems operate autonomously or in tandem... but taking even one of them out has to fuck with the Russian plans. If they didn't need two systems to achieve their objectives, there wouldn't be two systems in theatre."

Wheatcroft swore under his breath. He cast a last futile glance about him as though an alternative might be found, and then his shoulders slumped. It was a no-win situation. "Okay. Concur. We take the system out, and then we take our chances with the enemy IFVs and infantry."

Elway nodded and Colonel Wheatcroft closed his eyes. His decision amounted to a death sentence for every man in the Platoon.

*

Elway drew the Platoon close around him.

"We've got no choice but to fight these Russian bastards," he said quietly and urgently, looking at each soldier in turn.

"That big truck in the distance is an enemy EWS system that can fuck with the Allied attack headed towards us. We have to take it out. But once we do the Russians are going to come for us and there's no way we can evade them. So, we're going to make a stand right here and fight 'em."

Elway glanced sideways at the Colonel to see whether the senior officer had anything to add. Wheatcroft crouched lumpen and doughy-faced. He remained silent. Elway ordered the men to spread out along the riverbed and take up firing positions, then went along the line whispering to each soldier in turn, "Do not fire under any circumstances until I give the order!"

When he was satisfied that he had done all he could to defend their perimeter, Elway drew Sergeant Moon to him.

"Joe," he used Moon's Christian name deliberately, "We have to take out that Krasukha 8x8. We've got two AT4s to do the job. I want you and one other soldier to follow the riverbed east until you can circle around the Russian position, get past the trees blocking our line of sight, and take a clean shot. Who do you trust with the other AT4 to get the job done?"

"Give me 'Tinker', sir."

Elway nodded. Molly 'Tinker' Bell was a slightly-built black woman in her early twenties who had been born and raised in Springfield, Illinois. She had joined the US Army as a teenager, initially with the Transportation Corps before transferring to the regular infantry. Since joining Bravo Company, she had proven herself on the battlefront as a hard-working frontline soldier.

"Okay. You and 'Tinker'... but don't fucking miss, otherwise we're all gonna die for nothing."

*

Sergeant Moon and rifleman Bell went east, following the dry riverbed, moving silently and cautiously with the AT4s slung over their shoulders. After a hundred yards the shallow gorge kinked to the north and Moon paused for a moment to check his line of sight to the Krasukha 8x8 truck. From the lip of the riverbank, he could see the rear of the truck framed between two trees. The vehicle was an outlined halo of light in the viewfinder of his ENVG-B goggles, surrounded by a dozen or more men who were clambering over the vehicle and moving about nearby, preparing to leave the area. The four Russian APCs were parked nose-to-tail on the far side of the forest clearing, their shapes partially obscured by the bulk of the huge truck. The rear doors of IFVs were open and Moon saw the Russian infantry lining up into short files, waiting to embark.

Moon ducked down and drew Bell close to him. "We'll fire from here," he decided. "The Russians are preparing to move out. They're loading infantry aboard the troop carriers. The truck is going to have to make a three-point turn if it's going to head back out of the woods the same way it came in. That's when we open fire – the moment the truck is broadside to us and about to drive away."

They unslung the AT4s, uncovered the steel sights on their weapons, and when they were ready, they crawled to the lip of the riverbank, positioned about twenty feet apart. Moon slithered over the rim of the crest and took up position in the long grass, lying prone with his legs almost at a forty-five-degree angle to the target. Molly Bell found a gentle depression in the ground and dropped to her knee, the AT4 propped and balanced on her shoulder.

The range to the Krasukha was about two hundred yards; not a long shot for the AT4. The only challenge was the web of tall trees partially obstructing their view. Moon took a long settling breath and let the tension ooze from his shoulders. The ground beneath him was damp, seeping through his uniform. He heard the 8x8 truck's diesel engine bellow to life and blinked sweat from his eyes.

Moon and Bell watched and waited patiently. Two of the Russian IFVs made tight turns in the clearing and began to crawl east, their slitted headlights casting out thin glowing ribbons to light the way. Once they had moved off, Moon suddenly saw the shape of two more Russian troop transport trucks. They had been concealed until this moment by the bulk of the IFVs. One of the trucks moved away to the east in low gear, following the two IFVs. The rest of the vehicles in the clearing waited, diesel engines throbbing, while the driver of the 8x8 began to turn the big vehicle around.

Rifleman Bell felt for the trigger of the AT4 with her right thumb and left it poised there. She had the rear of the truck in her sights but as it turned, more of the vehicle became presented to her. She counted off the seconds, unaware that she was holding her breath. The truck turned with the aching slowness of a supertanker on the ocean, its blunt snout swinging with infinite sluggishness until suddenly − for just a heartbeat − it was exactly broadside.

Sergeant Moon shot first and a heartbeat later, rifleman Bell fired.

The two projectiles exploded from their AT4 launch tubes and skidded across the woods on wavering feathers of grey smoke. Less than a second after being launched, both projectiles slammed into the side of the Russian truck. The flash of the dual explosions lit up the night for an instant in a lurid orange glow as the roar of the near-simultaneous explosions hammered against the sky like successive thunderclaps. Then the view of the mangled truck's chassis was obscured by a billow of black smoke.

Rifleman Bell threw down the used launcher tube and dashed back along the riverbed towards the waiting Platoon, her boots splashing in the water and her heart thumping loudly in her chest. Sergeant Moon lingered on the verge of the riverbank for a moment until the roiling smoke shroud that was draped over the enemy truck began to lift. The two projectiles had utterly destroyed the rear section of the truck which contained the vehicle's huge dish and sensitive electronic equipment. The vehicle was on fire and canted to one side, a twisted wreck of blackened steel. He discarded the now-useless launcher tube in the long grass and slithered backwards until he felt himself slip down the face of the riverbank into cover. He saw rifleman Bell ahead of him and he ran after her, bent double, unslinging his M4 and mentally preparing himself for the dreadful toll the Russians would extract.

Elway watched the two projectiles destroy the Krasukha and felt a savage thrill of triumph. The explosive flashes flared for just a second and then the truck disappeared behind a wall of black smoke.

"Hold your fire," Elway warned the Platoon, speaking just loudly enough for every man to hear his orders. He had no need for such caution; the rumbling echo of the twin explosions concealed the lift of his voice. He waited. There was a long moment of stunned silence, and then suddenly the Russian infantry were spilling back out of their IFV's like an angry swarm of disturbed hornets. Officers screamed orders and men ran in different directions in confusion. A gunner aboard one of the IFVs fired his autocannon wildly into the night, lighting up the clearing with the flaming muzzle-flash of his weapon for several seconds.

"Steady…" Elway waited. He needed the Russian infantry out of their vehicles before he would give the order to shoot. Whilst ever the enemy troops remained in their IFVs, they were immune to small arms fire. "Steady…"

Through the clearing, Elway could see the Russians forming up amidst the choking smoke. More men appeared from beyond the burning truck until Elway figured there were around a hundred enemy soldiers. Some were formed up towards the west. Others began moving south, directly towards the river where the Americans lay in ambush.

Two hundred yards…

Elway waited, resisting the urge to open fire too soon. The Americans carried just a couple of spare magazines each. He needed the Russians to come closer to be sure every shot would count. Along the riverbank the Americans anxiously ran through last-second weapon checks, muttered silent prayers and held their breath.

"Steady…"

The Russians came on in skirmish order, stepping purposefully and fanning out as they advanced, putting space between each other. Elway figured there were at least seventy Russians in the ragged enemy line. They were dressed in camouflage fatigues. Some of the enemy soldiers seemed to be wearing night-vision aides, but most did not. At the left edge of the line the Americans heard an officer barking furious orders. Elway swung his M4 onto the man and singled him out as the first to die.

"Fire!"

Elway put a bullet into the Russian officer's head from a range of less than a hundred yards as the grassy verge of the riverbed suddenly erupted in hammering noise and spitting flame. Elway's bullet caught the Russian officer in the mouth, snapping the man's head back violently and tearing a fist-sized chunk of matted hair and grey custard-like contents out the back of the man's skull. For a hundredth of a second the Russian's head was distorted by the shattering impact, swelling, then bursting like a ripe melon. He fell to the ground like he had been jerked off his feet by an invisible length of tethered rope.

The opening fusillade stunned the Russians, hurling them down in a tideline of broken bleeding bodies. The range was so close it was all-but impossible for the Americans to miss, each enemy soldier lit bright in the viewfinders of their sophisticated night-vision goggles. The sounds of bullets thwacking meatily into the enemy carried above the sudden shouts and exclamations of panic. Some of the enemy soldiers dropped down into the long grass and began to return fire, spraying bullets wildly into the dark night. Their only reference was the flickering muzzle flashes of the American guns. Bullets fizzed thick in the air and streaks of tracer arced across the sky. One Russian threw a grenade ahead of him, but it landed well short of the riverbank and exploded in a harmless flash of light and upheaved earth.

"Keep shooting!" Elway urged his troops to maintain their rate of fire. He had achieved the element of surprise, catching the Russian infantry in the open and unguarded. The next few seconds of the firefight were vital.

A handful of enemy soldiers turned and fled into the distance. Sergeant Moon shot one Russian in the back and then caught sight of another enemy soldier creeping forward in the long grass to his right. Moon's face was fixed and masklike, as if he had detached himself from all emotion, leaving only the hands and eyes and ingrained skills of a trained machine as he went ruthlessly about his craft, his fingers working the M4s trigger, and his expression barely registering each new death he caused. He shot the approaching Russian in the head and saw the soldier's outlined shape go suddenly still.

"To our right!" Moon barked. He could see more men moving laterally through the grass, seeking the cover of nearby trees. "Watch the fuckers! Here they come!"

Molly 'Tinker' Bell and two others were at the far end of the Platoon's short line. The three riflemen all fired in unison. Two of the enemy soldiers went down, and a third threw his arms in the air and pirouetted, shot in the shoulder and thrown off balance by the brutal impact. Bell put a second round into the Russian, hitting him in the groin. The bullet-strike folded the enemy soldier forward and he sagged to the ground in slow motion, the agony on his face hidden by the night but the wailing scream in his throat piercing and shrill with wretched agony.

The night filled with confused angry voices and the whip-crack of small arms fire. Elway emptied his magazine, reloaded with swift economical movements, and shot a burly, muscled Russian soldier who had sprung to his feet from out of the long grass with his AK-74 on his hip.

It took three of Elway's bullets to put the Russian down but still he wriggled on, gasping with the effort, clawing at tufts of the stringy grass to haul himself forward. He was roaring in Russian; maybe urging his comrades on or cursing the Americans through the crippling waves of pain. He rolled onto his side and hurled a grenade towards the American line in a final savage act of defiance, then gasped his last breath and went eternally still.

The Russian grenade arced through the air and fell amongst the Americans with a deafening crash of thunder and a searing flash of light. Elway felt himself picked up and thrown backwards by the violence of the explosion, hanging in the air for a sickening moment and then crashing to the ground on his side. Clods of earth and rock rained down on him. He lay still for a mind-numbing instant and the battlefield around him seemed eerily silent. He shook his head and the clamor of combat returned to overwhelm him.

Elway groaned and pushed himself up into a sitting position. His face was burning. He pressed at his cheeks with his fingertips, and they came away bright with fresh blood. More blood spilled from his nose and ran into his gasping mouth, turning the dust there into a coppery-tasting gunk. He spat the filth from his mouth and felt himself sway like a boat on a storm-tossed ocean. His helmet had been ripped off his head by the force of the explosion. He groped in the dark until he found it in the trickling stream.

Through the lenses of his NVG-B goggles he saw carnage and devastation all around him. Three more Americans were down, one of them writhing and screaming in the smoke. Elway staggered to his feet. The nearest man was laying with his knees drawn up tight to his chest, the pants of his fatigues sheeted with blood. Another man lay face down in the water, his arms outflung and his lifeless head bobbing. The third figure was that of a woman. Rifleman Sally Bortha had been struck in the face and neck by shrapnel. She lay folded over, slumped against the riverbank, her expression in death blessedly serene and peaceful despite the obscenity of her gaping wounds.

Elway fumbled for his M4 and manfully staggered back to the lip of the riverbed. The firefight continued to rage all around him. He peered into the night, fired twice at the figures of two retreating Russians, and missed both times.

The enemy began falling back and, in their place, two of the enemy IFVs came crashing and jouncing through the undergrowth, closing on the riverbank to decide the battle. In the distance to their east, Elway heard and saw the other two Russian IFVs and the truck filled with Russian troops that had crawled away into the night returning at speed. The vehicles had been alerted by the tremendous clamor of the battle and had re-traced their route, appearing in the night through a palisade of trees, still several hundred yards away but closing quickly.

"This is where the shit hits the fan," Elway heard someone along the line mutter darkly. But it was not the only voice. Other men were venting their own fears and apprehension as a sudden sense of foreboding and unease washed over the doomed Americans

"Fitz! Where are you, man?"

"Ammo! I fuckin' need ammo!"

"Hollohan's dead: He's fuckin' dead!"

Elway looked sideways and saw Colonel Wheatcroft. The Colonel had lowered his M4 and was staring numbly over his shoulder at one of the men who had been killed by Russian gunfire. The young soldier had been shot in the face and thrown back by the bullet's impact. His head was a gruesome debris of shattered bone and blood, the wound so savage that the young man was unrecognizable beneath the ruined mask of his remains.

Wheatcroft shuddered, and then turned slowly until he had eyes on Elway. He licked dry, cracked lips and his mouth was thick with congealed saliva as he muttered, "I think we need to surrender."

Hank Elway flinched, then recoiled. "Sir?"

"I think we need to surrender," Colonel Wheatcroft repeated. The two Russian IFVs were closing quickly, their steel tracks flattening the grass as they bore down on the riverbank. Behind them and running crouched, were more Russian troops. The enemy armored personnel carriers were BMP-2s. They braked to a halt two hundred yards from the rim of the riverbank, their steel hulls yo-yoing on their suspension as they stopped suddenly, and their conical turrets turned. The returning Russian IFVs to the east continued to close on the battlefield remorselessly. In a matter of moments all four Russian troop carriers would re-join and fresh enemy troops would enter the fight.

The BMP-2s were fitted with night vision equipment and infra-red searchlights.

"We've still got ammo and we're in good cover," Elway was appalled at the notion of surrender. "We've given the enemy a bloody nose and we're still in the fight. We can't just give up now!"

But Wheatcroft seemed not to hear Elway's desperate plea. In his mind the Colonel was imagining the hammering scythe of the Russian 30mm autocannons mounted atop the enemy vehicle turrets. He visualized the murderous plunder those brutal machine guns would wreak from close range and he quailed. Tiny insects of fear crawled across his ragged nerves and itched beneath his skin. Death seemed inevitable and imminent.

"We'll take our chances in a POW camp," Wheatcroft gnawed at his bottom lip, watching the turrets on the BMP-2s turn menacingly, then turning his head to gauge the approach of the other two troop carriers and the truck crammed full of fresh enemy infantry. "It's better than being dead," he gave Elway a furtive glance and saw the outrage on his Captain's face. He rushed to mollify Elway, but his voice sounded like the whine of a petulant child. "We've achieved our mission. The Krasukha has been destroyed."

The mere idea of surrender galled Elway. He spat a mouthful of grit into the grass. "I'd rather we take our chances escaping, Colonel," Elway's tone turned blatantly defiant. "At least then we'd go down fighting. Good soldiers don't surrender, and these troops deserve better than to be carted off to some fuckin' Siberian slave labor camp... or shot in the back of the head by the side of a road."

In the distance Elway could hear Russian officers barking orders and he saw the infantry peel out from behind the cover of the BMP-2s and begin to stolidly advance. He ignored the approaching danger. "There's no guarantee that surrender will save our lives," Elway snarled. "The Russians might just line us up against a wall and shoot us. Look what we've done to their troops. We've killed dozens of them. You think they'll just accept our sudden surrender? They'll be in a murderous mood, and they'll want revenge."

"The Geneva Convention –"

"Isn't worth wiping your ass on in a combat situation," Elway's voice lashed cruelly.

"You're wrong…"

"Those bastards want to flay our guts!" Elway cut the Colonel off. "They'll just as likely murder us in cold blood!"

Wheatcroft shook his head. His mind was made up. He threw down his M4 and tentatively raised his hands into the air. As he opened his mouth to offer his surrender to the Russians, a shot rang out of the night, and the Colonel was struck in the forearm. His shoulder snapped back as if wrenched from its socket and then he slithered, screaming in pain, and gushing fresh blood, back down the slope of the riverbank.

Elway gaped in white-faced horror. But before he could gather his wits and give the order to open fire, another deafening retort suddenly boomed across the battlefield. It came from the opposite side of the clearing, manifesting as a sudden flash of light and then a thunderclap of noise.

The BMP-2 closest to the American position suddenly blew apart as if struck by a bolt of lightning. The vehicle was enveloped in a white-hot flash of light and then a tower of black boiling smoke. Shards of twisted metal scythed through the air as the vehicle's sides were ripped open, and its chassis wrenched in half. Three Russians close to the destroyed vehicle were immolated in the fierce fireball and another man fell into the grass, clutching at his leg and screaming.

Hank Elway stared in stunned disbelief and then heard a defiant distant voice lifted in a shrill battle cry.

"*Offenes Feuer! Tötet die Russen!* Open fire! Kill the Russians!"

Chapter 6:

The Company of German infantry emerged from the far tree line, moving with the purpose and discipline of hardened veterans.

Hauptmann Kurt Wolf, commander of A Company, 371st Panzergrenadier Battalion, swung his HK416 onto a Russian soldier standing in the forest clearing and fired twice. The H&K assault rifle was the standard weapon of the Bundeswehr. The light-weight weapon chambered the 5.56x45mm NATO cartridge and was used by several other Allied army units, including the Norwegian Armed Forces, the French Armed Forces and the US Navy's SEAL Team Six.

The Russian soldier that Wolf had fired at sagged at the knees, his face white with shock and his mouth hanging open. Wolf ran past the dying Russian, waving his men forward, urging them to close the range to the enemy.

The Russians were pinned between the American Platoon holding the riverbank and the German Bundeswehr at their rear. The surviving Russian BMP-2 in the clearing turned on its tracks, sideswiping a sapling to face the German surprise attack. The gunner in the turret opened fire with the vehicle's autocannon but a heartbeat after the first bullets began thrashing the air around the advancing Germans, one of the Bundeswehr dropped to his knee and fired on the BMP-2 with a Panzerfaust. The Panzerfaust was a lightweight, shoulder-fired, unguided anti-tank weapon used by the German Army. A milli-second after the operator squeezed the trigger the projectile's rocket motor ignited, sending the missile flashing across the forest clearing. The range was less than five hundred yards, and the BMP-2 was lit up by the fiery glow of its autocannon's muzzle-flash. The operator saw the projectile fly straight and true through the Panzerfaust's UP-7V telescopic sight, following the trail of grey wispy smoke until the front of the Russian IFV was suddenly enveloped in a wicked flash of light and a bloom of black smoke. The BMP-2 burst into flames that leaped from a rent torn in the front hull armor. The vehicle's hatches were thrown open and the crew of the IFV emerged screaming and consumed in licking fire. One man fell to the grass writhing pitifully. The commander of the Russian vehicle fell thrashing to the ground and somehow managed to jam the barrel of his sidearm down his throat, ending his own life and cutting his wretched agonized screams short before he was cruelly burned alive. The sound of the bullet whiplashed across the darkness.

The German infantry came on, roaring their battle-cry. The Bundeswehr veterans charged across the forest clearing, firing from the hip as they surged forward.

The Russian infantry spread throughout the woods turned in shock.

Captain Wolf pointed east and west, directing his men. "Watch those bastard IFVs to the east!" he shouted. "Hit them with the Panzerfausts!"

A handful of Germans broke from the attack and formed a thin line in the trees to the east of the heroic charge to fend off the approach of the returning Russian IFVs. A light machine gun opened fire on the enemy truck and two Bundeswehr dropped to their knees and fired anti-tank projectiles into the flames-lit night. One of the BMP-2s was struck on the front left track and disabled. The second vehicle lurched to a halt and fired its autocannon.

Another Panzerfaust fired, striking the second BMP-2 flush on the front hull. The projectile tore through the thin armor and exploded, killing the vehicle's crew and silencing the autocannon. The Russian IFV seemed to shudder as the projectile struck it, then a heartbeat later the vehicle blew apart in a roil of smoke and dust and debris.

"Kill the swine! Kill them all!" Captain Wolf heard the explosions away to his left and ran on. There was a gentle fold of ground ahead covered in a carpet of fallen leaves and tufted grass. The Germans threw themselves down into the shallow depression. A bullet fizzed just inches past Wolf's face. "Keep firing!"

The Russians did the only thing they could do; they dropped into the long grass and returned fire on the Germans.

The attack against the Americans was suddenly forgotten now the Russians were faced with a far more numerically dangerous enemy. A Bundeswehr Sergeant was shot in the shoulder, and he hissed a litany of unintelligible abuse as he went crashing to the ground. The man beside him reached for a field dressing to staunch the wound but was shot in the neck. He died instantly in a bright gush of warm blood.

"Feuer!" Captain Wolf shouted, as if the volume of his voice alone could urge his men to greater urgency. Russian machine gun fire cut through the night, winking red flashes of flame and for long unholy seconds the firefight reached a roaring crescendo. Grenades exploded in the dead ground between the Russians and the Germans, filling the forest with thick drifts of grey smoke.

A handful of Russians gathered their nerve and made a desperate charge towards the Germans, but they were cut down mercilessly. One soldier took a half-dozen hits and was almost cut in half. Another had his right knee shattered by a German bullet. He screamed in shrill agony for long seconds, dragging his maimed leg behind him as he tried desperately to crawl back into cover. One of the Bundeswehr lobbed a grenade that landed a few feet away from the crippled Russian. The soldier's body was flung cartwheeling through the air. He was dead before he hit the ground.

"Feuer!" Captain Wolf shouted again, then sprang to his feet and bounded forward until he was less than a hundred yards from the closest enemy soldiers. The Russians were being squeezed in a vice. They looked east and then west for an avenue of escape through the drifting smoke, but Wolf had foreseen the move; there were German light machine guns in the grass. The moment the Russians showed themselves the Germans opened fire.

With Colonel Wheatcroft laying wounded, Elway took command of the American troops. He lifted his head above the lip of the riverbank and saw the Russians beginning to reform. Shapes rose out of the long grass like ghosts fighting on stubbornly as the Germans continued to close on them. The fear here for Elway was that the Bundeswehr might be struck by errant bullets if he opened fire, so instead he ordered his men to hurl grenades. A handful of explosions shook the night and the ground around the enemy soldiers heaved. Clumps of dirt and tufts of grass were thrown into the air and the dust added to the haze of smoke until the shapes in the clearing appeared smudged and indistinct, even with the aid of NVG-B goggles.

Elway sent Sergeant Moon further along the riverbank with six men in the hope their fire could enfilade the Russian position. Moon and the handful of soldiers with him fired sporadically at targets of opportunity until the Germans mounted a final determined charge and overwhelmed the surviving Russians in a last furious frenzy of chattering gunfire and bloody screams.

The Bundeswehr showed the enemy soldiers no mercy, pouring fire into the hapless Russians until none were left standing.

Captain Wolf emerged from the smoke, his uniform spattered in blood, his face dripping sweat. A dark figure rose from the grass, the Russian's features gaunt and his eyes haunted with terror. He was bleeding from a chest wound. He tried to raise his AK, but his strength failed him. The weapon fell from his blood-slippery hands, and he staggered. He shouted a ragged cry of defiance in Russian, swaying on his feet. Captain Wolf shot the man between the eyes with casual indifference. The dead Russian fell to the grass and the sound of that last bullet echoed around the forest for long eerie seconds.

Wolf's lip curled as though he had caught the scent of something unsavory. "Russians. They are the filth of this world."

Elway and the rest of the surviving Americans slowly emerged from the cover of the riverbed. The battlefield reeked of smoke, tainted by the coppery odor of blood and gore. A German soldier who had been shot in the elbow rolled over in the grass and retched violently. Another German, his forehead crudely strapped with blood-soaked bandages, swayed on his feet and then collapsed. A Bundeswehr medic rushed to the man's aid.

Captain Wolf took off his helmet and wiped the sweat and spattered blood from his brow with the back of his hand. His eyes swung on to Hank Elway who stood, stunned, on the lip of the riverbank. "You seem to have a habit of finding yourself outnumbered in firefights, American." Wolf's voice was a mocking, superior taunt. "Battles you cannot hope to win on your own."

Elway recognized the Bundeswehr officer from the firefight at Glauben Sie Stadt. A moment earlier he had been about to hail and praise the Germans for their timely attack that had saved his men, but the German's churlish tone had incensed Elway. He turned on the Bundeswehr officer, his hackles up. "We wouldn't be in this situation if we weren't forced to do your work for you," he jabbed. "We just destroyed one of the Krasukhas your Company has been searching for," he indicated the smoking ruin of the 8x8 truck – "and risked our god-damned lives in the process. Maybe if you and your men were a little more competent…"

Wolf bridled, but his gaze remained mocking and arrogant. He shrugged aloofly, and surveyed the battlefield again, his eyes roaming over the smoking ruins of the Russian BMP-2s, and the dozens of dark crumpled bodies that lay amongst the grass. "Why did you fight here?"

"I told you," Elway snapped. He pressed his fingers to his face. The blood there was crusting but the open wounds ached. His features felt swollen. "We attacked because we knew how important the Krasukhas were to the enemy's proposed assault – and we knew you were hunting them."

"You chose to attack?"

"Yes."

"You didn't stumble onto the Russian position and were then ambushed?"

"No," Elway retorted, galled at the suggestion. "We were sent out to patrol the woods. We saw the Krasukha, and I convinced my Colonel that the system was critical to Russia's planned advance and a danger to the approaching Allied counter-attack. We were prepared to die to take the system out."

Wolf arched his eyebrows and his attitude changed in an instant. The arrogant tilt of his head disappeared, and his mocking tone vanished. He looked at Elway and the ragged remnants of the American Platoon with renewed respect.

"Where is your Colonel?"

Elway gestured with a jut of his jaw. "He was injured. He's over there."

"I must thank him for his heroic efforts."

Hank Elway said nothing, remembering the moment Wheatcroft has insisted the Americans surrender; remembering too the instant when the Colonel had actually raised his hands before being shot. Instead, he stared at the Bundeswehr Captain with a questioning look. "Did you destroy the second Krasukha?"

The German officer shook his head. "No. We still have not located the system," he sounded bitter and frustrated by the failure. "And now…" he glanced at the remaining men of his Company, "… I fear our losses have been too heavy to continue. We will return to base. Perhaps another unit will hunt for the Russian system."

"But there's not time −" Elway cut short the loud exclamation of protest, aware that he was on the verge of revealing classified information not known to the troops about the imminent Allied armored thrust that was preparing to crash into the Russian line.

Wolf seemed to sense what Elway had left unsaid. He shrugged his shoulders again. "There are a dozen woods and forests between here and the Oder River the Russians could be hiding in. Even if I still had a full Company, we could not search them all before sunrise."

"Damn!" Elway's bitterness was a raw lump in his throat. *Had he and his men fought and died in this forest for nothing?*

Wolf slung his assault rifle and strode towards the riverbank; his brow creased into a thoughtful frown. He glanced over his shoulder one last time and studied Hank Elway covertly for a long moment, then slid down the slope to the riverbed. There were a handful of wounded Americans lying amongst the rocks. One of the hovering medics pointed the German to where Colonel Wheatcroft sat, propped against the slope of the gulch with his arm in a sling. The Colonel's face was grey as ash, his eyes red-rimmed from fatigue and pain.

Elway and the rest of the Platoon walked amongst the dead Russians, turning bodies over in the grass and checking their pockets for documents. The officer Elway had shot to start the firefight was a Major, but apart from identity paperwork and a crumpled ticket of some sort, he carried no useful information. The surviving German troops dropped wearily down into the long grass and the soldiers from both Armies slipped into companionable camaraderie, sharing bottled water and cigarettes. Most of the Germans had a smattering of English but none of the Americans spoke German, so the exchanges between the troops became elaborate mimes while the medics continued to work at a frantic pace, their efforts punctuated by brief screams and rattling sobs of agony.

*

"The Colonel wants to see you, sir," Joe Moon plucked at Elway's uniform sleeve.

Elway heaved himself to his feet out of the long grass. His body was stiff. He felt like he had a shirt full of bruises. A medic had superficially attended to his abrasions and now half his face was swathed in gauzed bandage. Before he strode away, he asked the Sergeant for a butcher's bill.

"Seven dead, sir," Moon said with regret. "And four wounded. Rhee is unlikely to survive the return trip to Schwedt."

Elway grunted. The cost in lives for the destruction of the Krasukha had been high, but it could have been much higher. Tim Rhee was an Asian-American rifleman of Japanese descent. Elway made a pained face – Rhee was a good soldier.

Elway slid-skidded awkwardly down the incline of the riverbank and found Colonel Wheatcroft still talking to Captain Wolf.

The Colonel looked up when he saw Elway approach and the conversation stopped. Wheatcroft shifted position and wrenched his face into a grimace as a fresh stab of pain shot down his wounded arm. His eyes flittered, evasive and uncomfortable, his gaze clouded with the shadows of his personal shame. He had been about to surrender to the enemy and Elway had witnessed that act of cowardice.

"Captain Elway, I want you to select twenty soldiers still fit for combat," Wheatcroft spoke in a brusque bluster. "You will attach yourself to Captain Wolf's Bundeswehr Company and continue the search for the second Russian Krasukha. Leave our wounded and the German wounded here with me. I'll inform Brigade of your orders."

Elway flinched and for one unholy moment his face flushed red with outrage. "You're telling me to place myself and my men under Captain Wolf's command, Colonel?" Elway was appalled at the notion.

"No," Wheatcroft made an irritated gesture of appeasement. "I'm telling you to attach yourself and twenty men to the Captain's unit to replace the Germans who have been killed or injured. *Hauptmann* Wolf has explained the dire nature of his mission and assured me his orders come from NATO command. He has requested your support."

"Requested?"

Kurt Wolf nodded, his expression and his tone matter-of-fact. "You and your men are good soldiers. You're all veterans… and you understand the importance of what we're trying to do. With your help, we have enough men to continue the search for the second Krasukha. If you refuse, the search is over. And the entire Allied armored counter-attack might be at risk."

Elway thought quickly. The offer was an opportunity and a direct challenge. "We are out of ammunition…"

"The M4 uses the same NATO round as our HK416. We have plenty enough ammunition for your men," Wolf deflected the obstacle.

Elway nodded and the American and German Captains locked glances. Elway thought he saw an unspoken dare in the German's eyes. "Okay," Elway straightened his back and forced the numbing fatigue from his body.

The Bundeswehr officer smiled. He thanked Colonel Wheatcroft with a curt nod of his head and then shot Elway a sideways glance. "Be ready to move out in twenty minutes, American. We have much to do and no time to spare."

*

There was a small fleet of Marder 1A3 infantry fighting vehicles parked in a column on the northwest edge of the woods. The German and American infantry emerged from the treeline and Kurt Wolf directed the American troops towards the rearmost three vehicles in the line. The Marders were fifty-year-old relics from the Cold War that had served German Panzergrenadiere units since the 1970s. The vehicles were being phased out of the German military and replaced with new Puma IFVs. But every one of the new Pumas was on the frontlines, meaning the only mobile transport option Wolf and his men had to travel in the old Marders. The IFVs were heavily armored but could each only carry a handful of soldiers. The Marders were armed with an externally mounted 20mm cannon and a 7.62mm machine gun in a two-man turret. Onboard every vehicle was also a MILAN anti-tank guided missile launcher and reload missiles. Elway had never seen the German troop carriers up close before. They resembled a light tank.

"It will be uncomfortable for your men," Wolf shrugged and drew Elway aside as the troops squeezed aboard their assigned vehicles. "You, however, will not be so inconvenienced, I assure you. You will travel in the command vehicle with me, Captain."

Elway nodded. "Where are we going?"

"East, towards the Oder," Wolf said airily. "There are woods closer to the Polish border. The Russians might have hidden the second Krasukha there."

Elway said nothing. He recalled the comment the German had made at Glauben Sie Stadt about searching for a needle in a haystack. It was apt, he decided. The truth was the Germans had no idea where the second Russian EWS was hidden, and they were in a desperate race against the clock.

"We move out immediately," Wolf gave the order. The vehicles rumbled to life and a plume of grey diesel exhaust stained the air. Elway and Wolf climbed the rear ramp of the command vehicle and sat opposite each other. The interior had been gutted and filled with a bank of high-tech comms gear. The only other man in the rear of the vehicle was a dour-faced young RTO who sat lumpen and concentrating in front of his radios.

The Marders leaped forward with a sudden violent jerk and quickly gained speed, their steel tracks churning the soft green grass and throwing up a spray of dirt and clods of earth behind them. They slewed around and began trundling east at high speed in the darkness. Inside the command vehicle Elway fought to keep his eyes open. His body was running on fumes and willpower alone. The ceaseless strain of combat and the nerve-stretching fear of the past twenty-four hours had drained him so that he slumped heavily on the Marder's steel bench, his body swaying and rocking with every jounce and lurch of the vehicle.

Kurt Wolf watched the American Captain with bright calculating eyes. His expression was detached and clinical. He saw Elway fighting to remain awake and he pitied the American; he could see the strain on Elway's face; the evidence of a man on the rack who had been stretched to the limits of his endurance.

"How long have you been fighting?" Wolf asked suddenly, lifting his voice above the growl of the vehicle's engine to make himself heard.

Elway prised his eyes open, but it took a moment for his gaze to focus. "A few weeks... may be a month," he shrugged.

"You came to Germany directly from America?"

"Yes."

"You left your wife? Children?"

"Yes. I have a wife and three daughters. You?"

The German scoffed. "I am far too handsome to be with just one woman," Kurt Wolf said deadpan.

Elway wasn't sure if the German was mocking him or serious. "Have you been fighting for long?" he moved the conversation back to firmer ground.

"I was at Warsaw," the German Bundeswehr Captain said with a lamenting, regretful shake of his head. "And I fought during the retreat west. We underestimated the Russians, I think. Their men are well trained, and they are ruthless in a fight. Normally a conquering army lacks some motivation, yes? It is easier for the man defending his homeland to fight with dogged determination because he has something to lose... but the Russians were ferocious, and their artillery? Oh, my God!"

Elway nodded, recalling his own nightmare experiences of cowering in a trench under the thrash and flail of massed Russian guns, but he said nothing. Wolf's grim features loomed out of the dark; his face lit by the dull glow of the electronic equipment. "If they attack... if they mount their assault against our flank before the Allied Division approaching from the west reaches us..." he made a helpless gesture with his hands and then drew a finger across his throat. "... they will drive us back to the gates of Berlin."

The Marder tilted forward then righted itself, throwing the two men temporarily off balance. As the convoy drew further east, the speed of the vehicles slowed, and they moved more cautiously.

Elway glanced at his watch. "I was told the Abrams and Leopards at the vanguard of the Allied counter-attack would reach us at sunrise," he said with no real enthusiasm. Nothing in war went to schedule.

Wolf grunted. "I hope you are right, but I —"

A sudden staccato of loud and urgent radio comms drowned out the rest of Wolf's comment. The German Captain turned his head sharply and the RTO clutched at his headphones and leaned forward, his face intense. The radio operator listened, then snatched off his headphones and held them out to Wolf. "Sir…?"

Kurt Wolf clamped the headphones over his ears and listened for several minutes, his expression changing until his eyes were sharp and his features fixed with a savage snarl.

"Danke! Ich verstehe. Wir werden umgehend nachforschen!"

When the transmission ended, Wolf crushed the 'transmit' button with his thumb.

The German officer snatched off the headphones and turned to Elway. There was a predatory gleam in Wolf's eyes, the hard straight planes of his face lit by the eerie glow of the communications equipment so that his features loomed out of the dark.

"We have a lead," the Bundeswehr Captain could barely suppress his excitement. "One hour ago, a Lutfwaffe Panavia Tornado fitted for SEAD (Suppression of Enemy Air Defenses) missions was mysteriously jammed by a high-powered enemy EWS system. The pilot was flying south to north along the Oder River when the incident occurred, and he was forced to abort his mission with electronic malfunctions. At the time, he was two miles south of a small border town named Kleine Grenzstadt.

Elway listened to the German and became caught up in Wolf's sudden ruthless enthusiasm. "Do you know this place – this Kleine Grenzstadt?" Elway mangled the pronunciation.

"I have never been there," Wolf admitted. He broke the train of his thought to order the Marder's driver to immediately change course and accelerate, and then continued his reply, "but Kleine Grenzstadt is well known to those versed in Germany's medieval history. The town is close to the Polish border; just a mile or two west of the Oder. The town is built on a steep hilltop that thrusts several hundred feet above the surrounding farmlands. Today there are just a few shops, a few dozen homes and a church, but in medieval times the rise had once been the site of a hilltop castle that dominated the landscape during the 13th and 14th centuries. During its time, the *'Adlerhorst'* bastion had been an impenetrable fortified citadel against marauding attackers. In the ensuing centuries the castle has fallen into disrepair and in its place a modest town has grown up around the ruins."

"It would be the perfect place to site the second Krasukha," Elway was thinking fast and trying to imagine the location. "The elevation…"

"Yes," Wolf said. "Now it becomes obvious."

"But surely if the Russians had occupied the town there would have been reports of fighting."

"No," Wolf shook his head. "The towns closest to the river were evacuated many days ago because Command feared the Russian attack was imminent. The Russians could have moved the Krasukha into the abandoned settlement after the civilians were all evacuated."

Elway frowned, then fired off the next critical question. "How far away are we from this town?"

Wolf turned and spoke to the vehicle's driver through the Marder's internal comms. "About twenty minutes."

"We can't go in all guns blazing," Elway cautioned. "Not until we recce the town and see what strength the Russians have."

"No, I agree," Wolf nodded. "I have ordered the column to move to a small forested area about two miles west of the town. We'll approach on foot from there and keep the Marders concealed, ready to support us."

Elway shook his head. "It would be better if we circled to the north to make our approach," he explained. "If the Russians have OPs or a picket line, they will be orientated towards the west; it's the direction they would expect an incursion to come from. If we approach from the north, we will have the element of surprise."

"Detouring to encircle the town on foot will cost us perhaps as much as an hour."

"It's a small price to pay if it saves lives and if we can launch an attack against an unprepared defense," Elway argued.

Wolf thought for a long moment, weighing up probabilities and risk. He nodded. "Very well, American. We will do as you suggest. We will leave the Marders in the woods and circle the town to the north to make our approach."

"God willing, the Russians – if they're in the town – will be sound asleep at their posts."

"God?" the German arched his eyebrows with bemusement. "You still have faith in an Almighty after all the death and destruction and defilement of this war?"

"Yes," Elway said simply.

"Then I am envious of your faith," Wolf said, his voice suddenly introspective and almost ashamed. "I myself no longer believe. Not after what I saw on the retreat from Warsaw."

"Faith in my training, my men and God are all I have," Elway shrugged.

"Then say a prayer for us all, American, and I hope God is listening to you," Wolf put steel back into his voice, "for soon we will need all the help we can get."

Chapter 7:

The Marders reached the wooded grove and the men piled out into the dark night, taking each vehicle's MILAN anti-tank guided missile launcher and reload missiles with them. The route to the north of Kleine Grenzstadt was across flat level farm fields intersected with irrigation ditches. Karl Wolf glanced at the lowering sky overhead. There was a sliver of moon low on the horizon, but its glow was obscured by cloud banks and grey drifts of smoke. The distant silhouette of the town loomed out of the night as a jet-black rise on the landscape. He could see no house lights; nothing to suggest that the town was occupied.

They set out on foot in a single file column for the first mile but as the town grew closer and the great granite mound seemed to rear up before them, they moved into skirmish order, each man well-spaced and advancing with their weapons ready and their senses alert for any sound that might be a prelude to danger.

The rocky monolith upon which the town was perched loomed out of the night and began to gain definition. Elway gaped with quiet awe. The rise thrust a full two hundred feet above the landscape, like some great extinct volcano. The lower slopes of the craggy rise were tufted with clumps of bush and stunted, gnarled trees. Higher up the steep slope the rock façades became almost sheer in some places. The entire up-thrusted land mass was steeped in dark shadow so that only the edges of the crags showed in the ambient light of the night.

Elway saw a single road winding its way up the western face of the slope, zig-zagging in a series of sharp switchbacks as it snaked its way to the summit.

"The *'Adlerhorst'*," Wolf pointed. "The Eagle's Nest, as it was once known. You cannot see it from here at night, but the eastern slope of the rise still bears some of the ancient stone walls of the medieval fortress that once stood in place of the township."

Elway nodded and quietly quailed. If the town occupied by the Russians, it was going to be a nightmare mission to scale the slopes and fight their way through the cluster of buildings crammed atop the crest. To the American it seemed like a task more suited to mountain-climbers than infantry.

"It will be precisely our luck that we make the effort to assault the town only to find it is abandoned with no sign of the Russians," Wolf said dryly.

"Part of me hopes you are right – and part of me hopes you are wrong," Elway noted. "If the Russians are not in the town, we will have wasted our one last chance to destroy the second Krasukha EWS system… but if they are there, and if they have a couple of IFVs and a machine gun or two – we're going to die before we ever reach the town. Hell, the Russians could fight us off with a handful of rocks."

"Then pray for the third choice, American. Pray to your God that the Krasukha is in the town and the Russian soldiers are sound asleep."

The fact that it would be a night assault only made matters worse for Elway. He loathed night fighting; most soldiers did. Despite the advantage their sophisticated ENVG-B goggles would give the Americans, the fact was that night fights were chaotic, disorientating and confusing affairs that could turn to nightmare in a matter of seconds. It would only take a tragic blue-on-blue incident or perhaps an ambiguous order in the middle of a firefight for everything to go straight to hell.

A mile to the north of the town, the long skirmish line reached a drainage ditch that ran parallel to the rocky rise. The troops dropped down into knee-high brackish slime and took cover.

Elway paused to swallow a mouthful of warm water. "How do you want to play this?" he asked the Bundeswehr officer.

Kurt Wolf shrugged his shoulders. He peered into the night for long silent moments, his mouth working and his brow furrowed.

"The road runs from the west up into the town and it exits to the east where it crosses a bridge over the Oder," he was thinking to himself but speaking those thoughts aloud. "So, our best hope of subterfuge would be to continue circling around to the east and approach the town from the direction of the Russian Army. If the Krasukha is in Kleine Grenzstadt, the men in the town might assume we are a Russian relief column. But to approach from the east might mean crossing behind enemy lines. No doubt the Russians will have patrols closer to the Oder. It could be big trouble for us. The other option is to approach the town from the west because that is what the Russians will expect and be prepared for. Then if we could launch a second attack..."

Elway had been following the German's thought processes. He cast a glance skyward. Dawn was still some hours away but the smoke shroud that had hung in the sky from the long day of fighting was dissipating in the face of a nagging breeze. A soft eerie glow painted the surrounding landscape in a dull blue and deep indigo shadows.

Wolf rejected the notion of passing through enemy lines to make an eastern approach. There was no time, and the risk of being intercepted by a Russian patrol made the danger too great. He turned to Elway and there was a blatant challenge in his voice.

"How long would it take you and your men to climb the northern face of the escarpment?"

Elway blinked. "Are you serious?"

"Very."

Elway peered directly ahead into the ghostly glow of the night. The lower slope of the monolith rose at a gradual angle and was grassed and sprinkled with small trees, shrubs and boulders. He could not see clear details in the darkness, but he had the sense that the first part of the ascent would cause no great troubles. The higher the vast mound of granite rose, though, the steeper the climb would become. The upper reaches of the rock face were grey ragged slabs of stone, rutted and eroded into unpredictable shapes by millenniums of rain water runoff. Elway estimated the climb would take at least thirty minutes – if they remained undetected.

"At least an hour," he said.

Wolf grunted, then clenched his jaw, his decision made. "Very well. Your men will climb the north face and take up positions just below the crest of the rise. I will take my Company back to the west. In sixty minutes from now we will make an assault on the town up the road, firing to draw the attention of any Russian soldiers. At that moment you must launch your attack."

"That sounds fine in theory, but what if the Russians are up there in force?" Elway thrust an angry pointed finger at the crest of the rise where the little town was silhouetted against the sky. "We'll be slaughtered."

"The Russians will not be in force," Wolf was certain. "If they had a Battalion of troops up there our satellites would have detected them. Most likely it will be a similar-sized force to the one we encountered in the forest – perhaps a Company of regular infantry and two or three IFVs."

"Against twenty men," Elway reminded the German.

"Only for a short moment – if you do your work well," Wolf persisted. "As soon as you make your surprise attack, me and my men will storm up the road and meet you at the top."

"It sounds like a suicide mission…"

The German laughed, but there was no humor in the sound. "We are soldiers," he said simply. "Every combat situation is a potential suicide mission. And the risk is greater for my men," the German reminded Elway. "We will be the ones drawing the enemy's fire."

"If the Russians are in the town."

"If they're not," Wolf shrugged, "then everything we do will be for nothing."

Elway grunted. "Give me a couple of the MILANs."

"You'll never carry the weight of them up the slope," Wolf shook his head. "I will give you a couple of Panzerfausts instead."

"Okay," Elway nodded. Slowly his expression changed. The line of his unshaven jaw firmed, thrusting forward aggressively. At the same time he pulled his shoulders back and bunched his hands into tight fists. He was setting himself mentally for the challenge of the dangerous task ahead. He glanced at his watch, then, as an afterthought, ripped the gauze bandage from his cheek. The abrasions down the side of his face were still weeping and tender.

Elway went splashing through the water of the drainage ditch until he reached Sergeant Moon and the rest of the Americans. He filled them in quickly on the plan and they responded with grim, stoic silence. A flutter of wind flattened his uniform against his chest. Dark clouds were scudding across the horizon, blotting out the moon for long moments at a time.

"Okay," he took a long last breath and felt the adrenaline begin to fizz through his bloodstream; a potent cocktail of fear, uncertainty and reckless exhilaration. "Follow me!"

*

It began to rain; a grey veil of mist and drizzle that was pushed along by the breeze, so it hung over the farm fields and hollows like a blanket, smudging the silhouettes of the Americans as the moved through the long grass towards the foot of the rocky rise.

The men were sullen, disheveled and weary. They followed Elway in single file, their stomachs grumbling, and their heads hanging because they hadn't eaten or slept properly in two days. They looked like the damned, risen up from the ground, their faces sallow and corpse-like, their unforms thick with grime and gore as they shambled steadily closer to the base of the steep rise.

Half way across the fields of open ground Elway found a gully with steep grassy banks. It was as narrow as a trench and Elway supposed it was another dry streambed that had been cut through the landscape by centuries of erosion. He dropped down into the narrow channel and the men behind him followed. The temperature plummeted and the night turned bitterly cold. It seeped through the men's sodden clothing and frosted their breath. The wind sliced through them like a razor.

"We'll rest for five minutes and then push on," Elway whispered to Moon. He wanted the time to orientate himself and to make a precautionary scan of the lower slope. The last thing he needed right now was to run headlong into a Russian OP, hidden in the rocks and scrub. Normally he would have exercised far greater caution, but this night there was a deadline and high-stakes, so he must make do with a quick search of the ground ahead and trust his instincts.

The men waited, miserable and shivering. They huddled close together, wringing wet and pale faced. The rain grew stronger until it was drumming on their helmets and ricocheting off the rocks. The wind cut like the blade of a harvester's scythe. Moon produced an old camouflage-green kidney-shaped plastic canteen from within the deep recesses of his uniform. Elway arched his eyebrows in surprise. He hadn't seen a canteen since the Army had made Camelbacks standard issue.

Moon unscrewed the cap and passed the canteen under Elway's nose. "Rye Whiskey," the Sergeant looked hopeful. "I've been saving it for a special occasion. I reckon this might be as good a moment as any – with your permission, sir."

Elway almost smiled. He took a quick swig and felt the bite of the spirit in the back of his throat, burning its way warmly to his guts. He handed the canteen back to Moon. "Share it with the rest of the troops. God knows they need something to take their mind off the shit that is about to hit the fan."

The small canteen was passed along the line and came back empty. A minute later the Americans were on the move again, spread out in skirmish order now and moving forward bent-double, their eyes on the rubble of boulders at the foot of the monolith as they grew closer.

The Americans reached the base of the rise and melted into the rocks and scrub like ghosts. Elway glanced at his watch. Fifteen minutes had elapsed since they had separated from the Germans. He imagined the Bundeswehr troops moving away to the west and tried to estimate their current position. He figured they would be somewhere in the long grass on either side of the road that rose up to Kleine Grenzstadt, lurking there unseen in the rain and waiting for his signal.

The Americans set themselves to the climb. The ground around the foothills of the monolith was steeper than Elway had anticipated, and the driving rain made the ascent even more precarious. The wind's hooked talons plucked at the men, trying to tug them free of their handholds as they inched their way higher.

A rumble of thunder sounded and rolled across the cloud-filled sky. Elway peered up into the rain. He could see the crest of the rise through the mist and figured he still had over a hundred feet to climb. His arms were tiring and the rain-slick rocks beneath his clawed fingers were difficult to grasp. It was not a sheer cliff they were climbing, but it felt like it. In daylight, and in dry weather at a time of peace it would have been a pleasant Sunday afternoon adventure. At night, in the rain, with the threat of death just a split-second away, each step and foothold was filled with terrible danger.

Molly 'Tinker' Bell's face loomed out of the darkness, close to Elway's. Bell's teeth were gritted, her face wrenched tight with the effort of the climb. Directly above her one of the other soldiers lost his footing and slipped, his left boot hanging in mid-air. Bell thrust her hand up and caught the man's flailing leg, setting it back on the rocks. The man grunted an acknowledgement of thanks and scrambled higher, bringing a small avalanche of stones and dirt down on Bell and Elway. Bell spat out a mouthful of dirt and scraped her hand across her face.

"You good?" Elway whispered.

"Yes, sir," Bell rasped. "Basic was harder."

The Americans reached a rocky buttress where the stone was faulted in the form of a crude staircase. The route detoured around a bulge of overhanging cliff and lead to a small level ledge from where they could make their final assault on the crest. Elway went first. The route was strewn with gnarled tree roots, thicker than a man's arm. They sprang from the rock face like thick ropes and gave the men precious handholds as they wormed their way higher.

Below them, the ground dropped away precariously until they were inching diagonally across the face of the precipice with the empty void of darkness sucking at their heels. Elway paused to catch his breath and wedged his forearm into a deep crevice. They were just ten feet from a rocky crown that marked the crest of the rise. Elway pressed his mouth to the ear of the closest man and whispered.

"No noise from here on."

The word was passed along the line. Elway checked his watch. Fifty-five minutes had elapsed. He had two choices. He could get his men to the crest and pray he could find cover for them, or he could wait here, perched on the narrow ledge, and let the men rest briefly until the Germans opened fire. He was tempted to take the second option, but the wind and the rain made the notion of hanging there, clinging to the face of the cliff for a second longer than necessary, all but impossible.

"Catch your breath," Elway passed the word along in another chain of whispers. "I'm going to the crest to recce."

He went up the last few yards of rain-slick black boulders with relative ease, following a channel of rock with good footholds until his head and shoulder suddenly were rising above the crest and he had a view of the town.

Kleine Grenzstadt was just a fistful of small houses separated by narrow lanes and a single main road. The homes were white-washed stone and had high-pitched roofs. Most were bordered by low wooden fences. The nearest line of buildings were thirty yards away. Elway could just make out the sightless eyes of dark windows. He could see no lights burning. The whole town seemed eerily abandoned and for a moment he felt a profound sense of disappointment. If the town was occupied by Russians, he would have expected some signs of life; maybe a light, or the burble of a diesel engine or generator. He heard and saw nothing.

He spent a precious minute slowly scanning the dark clumps of bushes and the twisted shapes of trees, silhouetted by the night and then a chattering roar of noise tore the stillness apart.

*

"Attack!" Kurt Wolf watched the second hand of his wristwatch tick down and the moment it passed sixty minutes, he leaped to his feet and dashed forward. He leaped a grass-lined drainage ditch and ran along the blacktop, putting himself to the rise of road that wound up the hill to Kleine Grenzstadt. He fired as he ran, spraying unaimed bullets into the distance. In his mind a new clock started counting down, trying to calculate the response time of an enemy machine gun post. He ran fifty paces, his boots slapping loudly on the asphalted road, and then flung himself sideways into the cover of the long grass.

Nothing.

Wolf lay there, his lower body dangling in the water-filled drainage ditch, his upper body pressed into the soft wet earth. His heart was pounding in his chest and his lungs were pumping like a bellows.

Nothing but silence.

He crawled out of the ditch and rose cautiously to his knees in the long grass. He felt flushed and red-faced with foolishness. He paused for another ten seconds and then slowly clambered to his feet.

"Everybody up!" he gave the order.

The rest of the Bundeswehr Company rose from their concealment positions, emerging from out of the darkness, the tension drained from their bodies by the anti-climax. Wolf sighed and felt his shoulders sag with the weight of failure. He began to trudge forward. The men behind him drifted out of the grass and formed up on the road...

...which was when a flare suddenly exploded in the night sky and the entire Company of Germans were exposed under a glaring white light that silhouetted their shapes against the night.

"*Scheiße!*" Wolf swore bitterly "Fuck!"

The Russian machine gun posted on the roadside atop the crest suddenly opened fire, catching the Bundeswehr in the open. Wolf threw himself down on the blacktop and tried to make himself as small a target as possible. The machine gun hammered against the night, tearing chunks out of the road and filling the air with ricochets and jagged fragments. Two German soldiers went down screaming in the first furious seconds of the Russian fusillade. Then, mercifully, the flare died out and darkness draped itself back over the Germans.

"Disperse! Get into cover and return fire!" Wolf snarled. He was furious with bitter self-disgust. He had fallen for a Russian ruse and walked willingly – foolishly – into their trap. Now men were dying because of his mistake. "Get into the drainage ditch! Take cover!"

A second Russian flare wobbled through the air, reached the zenith of its trajectory, and then burst into a bloom of dazzling light.

In the sudden brilliant glare of its glow, the firefight began.

*

"Move your asses!" Hank Elway cried. "We're attacking now!" He heaved himself up and over the ledge and then lay prone in the rocky ground. The rest of the Americans clambered up the last few feet of the slope and lay either side of him. Two soldiers carrying SAWs set up at the ends of the line behind the cover of boulders to support the attack. Away to their west the chattering roar of gunfire intensified; a snarl and crack of machine gun and light arms fire.

"Go! Go! Go!" Elway was the first man to his feet, running forward crouching as low as possible. The rest of the unit bounded from cover to follow him, desperate to cross the thirty yards of open ground between them and the first line of houses. Elway felt the chill night breeze slash through his uniform that was drenched with sweat and soaked through from the downpour. Now he was in the open, the cut of the wind seemed even more ferocious.

Dark storm clouds still veiled the moon but a flare hanging in the sky lit everything for miles under its eerie glow. "Keep going! Don't stop until you are in amongst the buildings!"

They were half way across the open ground, caught in the middle of no-man's land, when the light suddenly struck them.

The brilliant glare of the search lamp cut like a knife through the darkness, blinding the Americans and illuminating them like they were in broad daylight. One man threw up his hands and seemed to freeze. Others dropped to the hard ground instinctively and rid themselves of their NVG-B goggles. Elway and Moon kept running. Elway pounded on with dogged determination, seething with bitter humiliation.

The Russians had been waiting for them and now they would die in a savage slash of machine gun fire.

The searchlight cast long sharp shadows across the broken ground and then a stutter of machine gun fire whipped and cracked through the air. The two American SAW operators reacted instinctively. They fired down the beam of the searchlight, their fingers jammed on the triggers, pouring hundreds of rounds into the darkness. The searchlight shattered and night crashed back down over the battlefield.

Elway reached the closest building and dropped to his haunches. He was breathing hard, each exhalation rattling in his throat. He turned and peered back across the broken ground. "To me! To me! Move it god-damn it!"

The Americans came on again, running into a hail of misdirected blind fire that criss-crossed the open ground from a couple of buildings to their right. Elway saw leaping muzzle flashes erupt through one house's broken windows and a split-second later he heard a man scream in pain. He swung his head in time to see one of the Americans cut down. The man's legs collapsed under him and his back arched. A handful more bullets struck the soldier. He was dead before he fell to the ground.

Elway raised his M4 and poured fire into the façade of the house where the Russians were, but it was an angled shot. His bullets tore chunks from the whitewashed stone wall and splintered the window frame. It was enough to force the gunmen into temporary cover, but nothing more.

The surviving Americans reached the first line of houses and crouched in cover. Sergeant Moon scrambled towards the building where the Russians had fired from and lobbed a grenade through the window. The entire wall of the small house seemed to blow outwards in an eruption of stone and debris and black smoke. Moon followed the blast of the grenade, bounding through the gaping hole and firing twice, killing the Russians inside. When he emerged back into the smoke-filled night, Moon gave Elway a matter-of-fact 'thumbs-up'.

Elway thought fast. His first priority was to locate and destroy the Krasukha EWS system.

He ducked his head around the corner of the house and scanned the narrow alley ahead. He could hear pounding footsteps and a confusion of strident shouts, but the lane was empty of enemy soldiers. That wouldn't last for long. The chatter of machine gun fire and the blast of the grenade Moon had just thrown were sure to bring enemy troops swarming towards them in the next few seconds.

"Follow me!"

Elway rose and went forward, hugging the wall of the lane with his M4 at his shoulder, all his senses heightened. His mouth was dry, the beat of his heart erratic, and his body numb with cold dread. Flashes of flickering light flared across the far end of the lane and then three Russian soldiers appeared, silhouetted against the orange light. Elway fired instinctively, aiming his shots. All three enemy soldiers were flung to the ground. Two of the Russians lay very still but the third writhed on the ground, screaming and howling. Elway ran forward and put a bullet into the enemy soldier's head. The cobblestones were spattered with blood.

The Americans reached the end of the lane. Another alley ran from left to right in a T-junction. Elway sent one squad of troops and one of the Panzerfausts west with Sergeant Moon and then led the remaining soldiers east. Before the two squads separated, Elway seized Moon by the sleeve of his jacket. "If you get a sight of the Krasukha, don't hesitate. Blow it the fuck up. It's the only thing that matters."

Chapter 8:

There could be no long-range firefight in an urban environment. Elway knew the fight for Kleine Grenzstadt could only be won as a blood-soaked fray, fought at close quarters.

"Keep your fuckin' eyes peeled!" he went forward along the narrow sidewalk of the laneway. From the maze of streets all around him rose the sounds of fighting and confusion. The night was lit up by flaming muzzle-flashes. Elway had no idea where the German Bundeswehr were, or even if they had yet managed to fight their way to the edge of the town. All he knew was that he had to find and destroy the Russian EWS system.

A clamor of percussive explosions sounded to his left and he dashed to the next intersection and peered around the corner. It was another laneway that seemed to lead towards the center of the town. The way ahead was veiled with roiling black banks of smoke. He paused for a moment and listened, the rest of the squad so close behind him that he could hear their hoarse breathing and smell the ripe odor of their sweat and fear. Another explosion sounded, this one seemingly coming from just beyond the smoke. He saw a brief stab of red flame and then a moment later rubble and debris were thrown into the air.

"This way!"

The squad went forward and burst through the smoke into a chaos of flames and screams and fury.

Bodies lay sprawled on the sidewalks and in the middle of the road. Most lay motionless, their blood running in rivulets into the gutters, but others stirred and groaned in agony. A Russian soldier wearing just fatigues and no body armor was on his hands and knees vomiting blood in a shattered doorway. Next to the man was another Russian. He was laying on his side with his hands clasped over his split-open guts. He was sobbing with the agony of his wounds, his heels tapping gently on the cobblestones as the life slowly seeped from him. Another explosion sounded and part of a house blew to pieces, filling the air with debris. Elway flinched and covered his head as rock fragments and splintered timbers fell like hail.

They were in some kind of cul-de-sac of town shopfronts. Several of the buildings had suffered damage and the road was sheeted with sparkling shards of shattered glass. A shot rang out from somewhere amidst the veil of smoke and one of the men behind Elway was spun around and thrown off his feet. The soldier collapsed to the ground clutching at his shoulder. More shots hammered, gouging chunks out of the wall above Elway's head. Molly Bell dropped to her knees to tend to the injured man's wound but Elway roared at her. "Leave him! We can't stay here. Keep moving!"

They dashed forward into the smoke, crouched low. Elway heard a stutter of small arms fire from somewhere off to his left and he followed the sound, his NVG-B goggles showing the outline of more buildings and then, between them, a wider stretch of road. He sensed they were nearing the center of the town, though how in God's name he had managed to stumble in the right direction was beyond his understanding. He was completely disorientated; turned around by the maze of alleyways and narrow lanes so that he was, in that moment, unsure of his direction or the location of Sergeant Moon's squad.

The laneway they were following curved abruptly to the left. Elway paused to peer around the corner. He could see the main street of the town now. There was a Russian IFV parked across the blacktop. The vehicle's autocannon was firing in short lethal bursts of hammering noise, the turret-mounted barrel spitting flames and venom that lit up the night. On the street surrounding the vehicle he counted at least a dozen Russian infantry. They were facing away from him, kneeling in the cover of doorways and firing from behind low stone walls, shooting, Elway presumed, at the advancing Bundeswehr. As he watched, one of the Russians reached for a grenade and sprang to his feet to hurl the explosive into the darkness. But the moment he revealed himself, a torrent of German small arms fire cut the man down. The grenade rolled from his lifeless fingers and exploded, adding more noise and smoke to the confused chaos.

Elway turned to the men around him and pointed ahead. "The Germans must be advancing along the road. That's who the Russians are firing at. We're going to take the enemy in the flank. Bell?"

"Sir?"

"Can you fire that fucking thing?" he pointed at the Panzerfaust Molly Bell carried.

"Absolutely," Bell said with confidence.

"Then don't fucking miss."

Bell dropped to her knee and braced herself against a wall. A German had given her a five-minute crash course on firing the weapon when it had been handed over. Bell took her time, going through the weapon's simple aiming and arming process, her mouth moving, and her voice hushed as though she were coaching herself through the steps.

"The instant that IFV is taken out, we follow the projectile, understand? The moment that fucking thing blows up, we move forward and hit the enemy hard," Elway filled in the brief moments of delay by issuing instructions to the rest of the squad.

The range to the Russian vehicle was perhaps a hundred and twenty yards. Bell waited until the vehicle began firing away into the dark again and then fired the Panzerfaust.

"Fire in the hole!"

Elway and the men in the squad clamped their hands over their ears.

The projectile leaped from the launcher and Bell was surprised by the amount of 'kick' the weapon had. The recoil rocked her back on her heels and squeezed her against the wall – but the projectile flew straight and true. The Russian IFV blocking the road erupted in a flash of flames and a huge cloud of smoke.

"Go! Go! Go!"

The squad bounded forward, spreading out and surging down the dark alley with their weapons blazing. The Russian infantry on the street were taken by surprise by the unexpected flank attack. One enemy soldier turned to fire into the alley, but he was cut down by the man at Elway's shoulder. Elway saw the rounds from the M4 stitch their way across the sidewalk and then hammer into the Russian's kneeling figure. The enemy soldier was hit several times, his body jerking erratically like he was being manipulated by a puppeteer's strings. The punching power of the M4 knocked the man over and killed him.

"Finish the bastards!" Elway snarled. Urban warfare was all about momentum and initiative. The small group of Americans had caught the Russians by surprise and the next few seconds, Elway understood, were critical. There could be no mercy. There could be no split-second of hesitation. Street-fighting demanded ruthless, ferocious savagery. "Kill them all!"

The squad burst through the entrance of the laneway and out onto the main street of Kleine Grenzstadt. Elway glanced left and saw the familiar figures of several German Bundeswehr breaking from cover and advancing to meet up with the Americans. He turned his head and peered into the smoke instead, trying to judge the strength of the enemy. The Russians had been slow to react to the sudden flank attack and the Americans were instantly amongst them. One Russian fired into the night, clipping an American and severing two of the soldiers' fingers on his left hand. The American roared, more in anger than pain. His momentum carried him forward. He fired a short burst from his M4 and hit the Russian soldier several times in the chest. Still the American surged forward, raising his M4 like a club and swinging it hard into the Russian's face. The enemy soldier's jaw shattered under the brutal attack and a spurt of bright red blood splashed the wall behind him. Then he was down on the ground writhing and screaming in blood-gurgling agony. The American planted a boot in the middle of the enemy soldier's chest to pin him to the ground and then shot him between the eyes.

The Russians broke from cover and began to withdraw east along the road. Elway was consumed by the red mist of a warrior's rage. The days of tension and anxiety, the hardship and deprivations, the nerve-shredding constant apprehension exploded from him in a savage roar. "Kill the fuckers!"

He dropped to his knee and fired at a Russian soldier who had just emerged from the dark shadows of a doorway. The retreating figure was lit up in the viewfinder of Elway's goggles, but even without the high-tech optical aids, there was enough ambient light from the surrounding burning buildings to throw the man's figure into stark relief. Elway fired twice, missing with his first bullet and hitting the man in the knee with his second. The Russian went sprawling to the ground, the AK-74 in his hands flying from his grip and skidding across the blood-soaked cobblestones. Elway sprang to his feet, bounded forward and shot the man from close range, then turned, wild-eyed, looking for another target. He could hear screams and shouts. He saw Bell fire three times at a fleeting figure, but he had no idea whether she hit her man. One of the Bundeswehr ran past him, charging down the center of the road with his weapon on his hip. Then a flurry of return Russian fire scythed through the air. A bullet fizzed past Elway's ear, missing him by mere inches, but the charging German was not as fortunate. Elway saw the man's head snapped back and for an instant he was enveloped in a red mist of blood. He fell to the ground. Elway stepped over the dead body and dashed forward. Other squad members and several Bundeswehr joined him, fighting shoulder-to-shoulder.

The Russians retreated from the savagery of the attack and melted away into the darkness. Kurt Wolf, his face drenched in a mask of spattered blood, caught up with Elway by the smoldering wreckage of the destroyed Russian IFV. There were blackened, charred bodies in the tangled ruin, and there were more Russian bodies close by, their uniforms singed from their bodies, their faces gruesome mangled messes. A dead German lay in the gutter and another was slumped against a stone wall, his head down on his chest like he was asleep.

Everywhere Elway looked there was blood and death. The air stank of something fetid and foul.

The battle fell into a momentary unholy lull and in the brief respite bleeding men tended to their wounds and others gulped warm water. The American who had lost two fingers clutched his injured hand to his chest and growled in snarling pain while a comrade mummified his hand and forearm with a thick roll of bandage.

"The Krasukha?" Karl Wolf's throat was so raw from shouting that the question came as a rasp between dry, cracked lips.

Elway shook his head. "No. You?"

"No sign of it," Wolf sagged, deflated, then noticed how few Americans remained. "Were the rest of your men killed?" Wolf's tone was sharp.

"No. We separated. Sergeant Moon has a squad."

"Where is he?"

Elway shrugged, then as an afterthought snatched the radio from his hip.

The town had fallen eerily silent, but the buildings continued to burn. Flames and showers of red sparks leaped high into the night sky.

"Six-Four, Six-Six. SITREP."

There was a long pause before the radio in Elway's hand crackled with a burst of static. "Six-Six, Six-Four. We're at the eastern edge of the town," Moon's familiar voice broke through the hiss, his voice unusually hushed and tight with tension.

"Contact?"

"Yes. We have eyes on the Krasukha! The Russians are preparing to pull the vehicle out of the town."

"Take it out!" Elway suddenly came alive with renewed urgency.

"Negative. We used the Panzerfaust on an IFV."

"Fuck!" Elway cursed. He turned and in a single long breath filled Wolf in.

"Tell your Sergeant to pin the Russians down until we fight our way to him," Wolf began waving his arms, marshalling the Germans.

Elway got on comms again and ordered Moon to open fire. "If that truck gets away, thousands of lives might be put in danger. Do whatever it takes to disable the vehicle. It can't be allowed to retreat across the Oder!"

*

Elway and Wolf dashed east with their men hard on their heels, using what scant cover the houses and shopfronts offered as they ducked and weaved and criss-crossed the street, bounding from building to building. In the distance ahead of them, they heard a sudden eruption of small arms fire followed by two explosions. The night sky lit up with a flickering fiery glow.

A Russian leaned out from behind the corner of a house and opened fire on the advancing allied soldiers. Bullets zipped and ricocheted through the air. A Bundeswehr Corporal was struck in the face and his head seemed to explode. The weapon the German was carrying clattered from his hands, and he rolled, dead, into the gutter. One of the Americans dropped to his knee and returned fire. The Russian was lit up like a beacon in the man's night vision goggles and the range was less than a hundred yards. The Russian was flung back by the impact of two bullets. He fell forward, across the narrow sidewalk gushing blood from fatal wounds.

Elway leaped over the twitching body of the dying enemy soldier and heard a raised Russian voice coming from behind a barricade of sandbags in front of him.

"*Otkrytyy ogon'!* Open fire!"

A fusillade of light machine gun fire erupted from the sandbagged bunker and the allied troops, hemmed in by the houses on their side of the street, were forced to scurry and scatter into cover. Some men threw themselves down prone onto the cobblestones and returned fire. Other men dashed laterally for the nearest door, the closest fence or bush.

"Christ!" Elway seethed. He ducked behind a low stone wall where Karl Wolf was crouched. Elway was breathing hard. "We've got to take the LMG out."

Just a few feet to their left and laying on his back with his arms spread wide and his open mouth crawling with flies was an old man wearing a threadbare black jacket and rumpled trousers. He had been shot between the eyes, evidently several hours earlier. His corpse was bloated with gasses, the flesh purpling and grey. Macabrely, the dead man's pockets had been turned out and one of his fingers was missing. Wolf sneered. "The Russians must have executed the old father and then ransacked the body for money and jewelry."

Elway could smell the corpse. The stench caught in the back of his throat; a sickly-sweet stink of corruption.

The Russian machine gun fired again, and a stream of bullets gouged stone shards from the top of the rock wall the two officers were cowering behind. The sudden roar of enemy bullets brought Elway's attention crashing back to the immediacy of his problem.

"We can outflank them easily," Wolf risked his life to steal a peak at the buildings on either side of the street. "There must be back yards. We can send men to circle around…"

"Too much time," Elway shook his head then settled on a more desperate idea.

"Get a half-dozen men together and give me covering fire," he began to set himself for a suicidal charge. He filled his hands with a couple of grenades.

Wolf passed a message to a nearby knot of men crowded in the cover of two doorways through hand signals, then slapped Elway on the shoulder.

"Go!"

Elway sprang to his feet like a sprinter out of the blocks, running directly towards the sandbags and into the snapping jaws of the enemy machine gun. The instant he broke from cover the Bundeswehr in the doorways unleashed a hammering fury of small arms covering fire, forcing the Russian machine gunner to duck as a solid wall of bullets cracked and snapped and socked into the sandbags. Elway ran on, then hurled the first grenade. It flew long and exploded behind the sandbagged wall, cracking apart in a flash of explosion and an eruption of black smoke but doing no damage. He pulled back his arm and slung the second grenade, then hurled himself sideways, diving towards a closed door. Elway hit the door with his shoulder and it burst inwards just as the second grenade plunged down on the enemy machine gun position. The grenade bounced on the cobblestones and then exploded. The two Russians crouched in cover were hurled into the air; their bodies shredded with shrapnel. The sandbag wall was torn apart, and the machine gun utterly destroyed. Elway staggered out through the shattered door and stood on the sidewalk for a moment, dripping sweat, and trembling from the exertion and the after-effects of his terror.

"Advance!" Wolf ordered the attack forward again.

The Russians fell back, and the Germans hunted them through the narrow blood-soaked lanes relentlessly. The attack lost all cohesion and broke down into a series of small savage skirmishes. Wolf and three of his men kicked down the front door of a house and lurched into a fusillade of Russian fire. A Bundeswehr Sergeant was shot in the shoulder and staggered back out into the street blood streaking his arm. But Wolf sidestepped the stutter of bullets that had been fired from behind a small kitchen counter. The German Captain ducked behind the cover of an internal wall and returned fire, crushing his finger down on the trigger, abandoning all weapons discipline. Bullets dismantled the house's kitchen, tearing plaster walls to shreds, shattering crockery and splintering furniture. Splintered fragments of wood flew like shrapnel and the Russian gunman was forced down into cover. Smoke filled the ground floor of the house and the noise in the confined space was a dreadful roar that stunned the senses. Finally, Wolf's rifle fell on an empty chamber and in the sudden eerie lull the soldier beside Wolf underarmed a grenade. The entire kitchen was consumed in a flash of light and an explosive crack that also punched a hole in the home's side wall. The Russian died hard, his body eviscerated and dismembered in a ghastly rupture of spattered blood and gore.

Wolf emerged back onto the sidewalk, spots of the Russian's sprayed blood on his cheeks and staining his uniform. He glanced at Elway; the German's expression fixed with grim resolve. "We move on," he said simply.

The last knot of resistance was at the eastern edge of the town where Russian survivors were dug in and making a final, desperate stand.

Elway ran towards the sounds of gunfire but pulled up abruptly at the corner of a building. Beyond the next bend, the street was a scene from a nightmare. Many of the buildings were ablaze and in the middle of the road, lit by the leaping flames, was the silhouette of the second Krasukha EWS system. Elway could tell instantly, even in the uncertain light, that the massive truck carrying the sophisticated Russian electronic system was damaged. The vehicle was down on one side and the monstrous dish atop the rear of the truck's chassis was tilted askew and streaked black. There was shattered glass strewn across the rubble littered street and more than a dozen bodies, their crumpled shapes lying lifeless amidst spreading pools of blood. The Russians were firing from several destroyed buildings, shooting into the night at Sergeant Moon and his squad of men on the opposite side of the road.

Elway sensed the battle was descending into a stalemate. Moon's small squad of men had not had the firepower or the numbers to maintain the momentum of their initial attack and the Russians had barricaded themselves, fighting stubbornly.

"We need to rush those buildings," Elway pointed ahead, indicating where the enemy's firing positions.

Wolf shook his head. "We need to destroy the Krasukha first," he insisted.

A Bundeswehr Sergeant stepped forward. He was a huge brawny man with an anvil-shaped jaw, a short crop of blonde hair, and a broad chest. The Panzerfaust in his massive hands looked like a children's toy. Wolf gave the Sergeant his instructions and Elway watched mutely while the soldier casually dropped to one knee, aimed the anti-tank weapon and fired.

The projectile streaked across the cobblestones, moving through the air too quickly for Elway's eyes to track. A hundredth of a second after the Sergeant squeezed the trigger, the 8x8 Russian truck in the middle of the blacktop exploded from a direct hit.

Even though Elway knew the massive blast was coming, the savage roar of the projectile slamming into the front of the truck and the fierce explosion that followed startled him. For a heartbeat the entire street was lit by the blinding flash and the sound on the night boomed and echoed across the sky.

Twisted shards of mangled metal were hurled hundreds of feet into the sky. Flames overwhelmed the truck, burning fiercely, gutting the cabin's spartan interior and melting the massive rubber tires.

"Now we can assault the buildings," Wolf said simply, the hard planes of his face lit up by the blazing inferno. "Now the threat to the Allied attack is neutralized."

The cluster of Americans and Germans gathered themselves in the shadows to make one final assault. Elway got on comms to Sergeant Moon and ordered his squad to hold their fire. But before the first grenades were thrown and before the German LMGs could hammer the façade of the buildings with covering fire, the Russian defenders suddenly emerged into the night, their hands raised.

The enemy soldiers looked like bedraggled refugees. Their eyes were huge and fearful, their faces streaked with grime and soot and sweat. They emerged into the smoke-filled night in single file, some clutching at wounds, others limping. One man came through the shattered door sideways with a comrade's arm slung over his shoulder, supporting the injured man who was bleeding from a gut wound.

The Germans dashed forward, shouting, their weapons raised. The Russians dropped submissively to their knees and threw their hands into the air, declaring their surrender and pleading for mercy.

The fight for Kleine Grenzstadt was over.

"Congratulations on successfully completing your mission, Captain Wolf," Elway was generous in his praise. "Bravo Company was proud to be of assistance to the Bundeswehr." Elway was so exhausted the gesture of merely extending his hand required a monumental effort. He remained upright only through stubborn force of will.

The Bundeswehr Captain flinched and recoiled as though Elway held a rattlesnake. "This is bad luck and premature," he glanced down at Elway's blood-stained hand. "We still have much to do."

"You're kidding," Elway frowned. His eyes swam out of focus with the potency of his fatigue and then sharpened. "We destroyed the two Russian Krasukha. The job is done."

"You think like a foreigner," Wolf made the comment sound like an accusation. "But I am a German. This is not just another fight. This is our homeland. And I say to you that there is much more we can do. Yes, we have destroyed the enemy's EWS, but we are behind Russian lines, and we hold high ground. In perhaps an hour or less the Allied push will stream from out of the west and crash against the Russian flank. But as soon as the first shots are fired, the Russians will seek to re-take Kleine Grenzstadt. From here their mobile missile launchers and anti-tank systems could wreck dreadful damage to our attack. So, we must deny them this position. We must bring up the Marders and we must dig in and defend the town and prevent the Russians from re-taking it."

Elway felt himself deflating and the waves of exhaustion came crashing down on him. He had nothing left to give; no more reserves of strength or energy to carry him through another long day of savage fighting. Wolf saw the play of emotions on the American's face; first the look of dismay and then bewilderment and finally despair.

"But first you and your men need food and rest." Wolf was not being generous – he was being practical. The Americans were no good to him in their current state, and if the Russians attempted to seize the town, he would need every available gun to fend their attack off. "Go," Wolf insisted. "Find food for your men and a place to sleep. There is nothing for you to do until the Marders arrive and we can find hull-down positions for them to defend the approaches."

"What about your men?" Elway's sense of fairness made him pause. He wanted no favors from the German. "I will rest my men too," Wolf conceded. He summoned his radio operator and ordered the Marders to break their woodland cover. "Tell them to move out immediately," Wolf gave the RTO precise instructions. "I want them here in the town before dawn."

The message sent, Wolf and Elway made a cursory inspection of the town's outskirts. The two men stopped beside the road that slalomed down the face of the rise and then ran west towards the far horizon.

"Very soon the skyline will be filled with our tanks and APCs," Wolf peered into the looming darkness as if he might see a smudge of dust cloud on the horizon. "And when the Russians become aware of our attack, they will move forward to intercept. It will be a very dangerous situation for their tanks and infantry. They will have the Oder at their backs, no room to maneuver, and just a few pontoon bridges to escape across. They will fight like cornered rats…"

Elway grunted, and then the two officers returned to the town, the American in search of food and rest, and the German eager for the attack that might free his country from the stranglehold of the Russians.

The mission to destroy the menacing Krasukhas was over – but the fight for the future of Germany was just about to begin…

Chapter 9:

The only clear advantage the Allied forces arrayed along the German-Polish border had over their Russian counterparts was superior intelligence. Fresh satellite updates and ELINT poured in to Allied Command Headquarters throughout the night, providing the NATO war planners with a clear picture of Russian dispositions along the battlefront.

This information was used to plan the Allied armored counter-attack, which, Command hoped, would crash against the enemy's flank and send the Russians reeling back across the Oder River; back into war-torn Poland.

The Allied scheme called for a Battalion of Abrams tanks to hit the Russian line two kilometers south of Kleine Grenzstadt and to drive a wedge between the enemy's positions. Then the forty-four Leopard 2A7s of the German 203rd Panzer Battalion tanks would strike from further to the north, crushing the severed section of the enemy line before turning to unite with the Abrams to roll up the rest of the shattered Russian flank.

The last great modern tank conflict was the Battle of 73 Easting which had been fought in 1991 in the Iraqi desert between Coalition armored forces and Iraqi armored forces. The battle for the future of Germany would be fought over very different terrain, and even the war planners themselves were uncertain of the outcome. The farm fields, rolling hills, streams and wooden valleys of north eastern Germany were a world away from the flat expanse of the Iraqi desert, meaning the looming tank battle would be fought at closer ranges and in the confined space of just a ten-kilometer stretch of battlefront.

*

Karl Wolf radioed Battalion Headquarters from his command vehicle and informed his commanding officer that the two Russian Krasukhas had been destroyed and that he and the Americans with him were preparing to fortify and defend Kleine Grenzstadt behind Russian lines. When he emerged from the rear of the Marder, Wolf was grim-faced with resolve.

"I've just been notified that the nearest Allied tanks are fifteen kilometers west of us," he explained to Elway. "They are being slowed by congested highways and the tide of civilian refugees streaming away from the battlefront."

"Fifteen kilometers?" Elway tried to convert the distance into a more-familiar measurement of miles, then looked troubled. "That doesn't give us much time to prepare a defensive position."

The men set about the task of turning the small town into a living hell for any Russians sent to seize the position. They began by building obstacles along the length of the main road, using furniture, rubble, concrete slabs and splintered timber beams to block the thoroughfare, concentrating on places where the blacktop narrowed and the houses on either side were relatively undamaged. Wolf and Elway inspected the work with bleak satisfaction. Any armored vehicle that reached the town's outskirts would be forced to slow to a crawl to negotiate the tight confines. Elway pointed to several nearby windows, identifying the best shooting positions. Wolf broke the survivors of his Company into small four-man teams and spread them throughout the battle-ravaged environment. Some positions were concealed behind mounds of broken bricks and rubble on street corners, but most were in elevated positions at the western end of the main street, from where his troops would have an unobstructed view of an approaching armored column. Wolf gave most of his time and attention to siting the MILAN anti-tank weapons and the few remaining Panzerfausts he had. Elway kept constantly checking his watch; he had a man with binoculars and a radio posted on the roof of a house on the western edge of the town.

Karl Wolf positioned the Marders in the ruins of several buildings along the main road and ordered the crews to camouflage the vehicles under layers of dirt and debris to disrupt their angular shapes.

When the work was finished and every preparation had been made, the waiting began...

"Six-Six, Six-One," Elway's radio sparked to life. "Dust on the western skyline."

"Are you sure?" Elway glanced to the sky. Dawn was just breaking; a pale glow of light rimming the far horizon.

"Confirm, Six-Six."

Elway broke comms and gave Wolf an ominous look. "The first allied tanks are coming into view."

The two officers dashed to the western edge of the town and peered into the distance. From the lofty perch of their position, they had an unobstructed view for miles in every direction. Slowly the darkness of night drew back, and each passing minute expanded the range of their vision. The Russian positions emerged first for they were closest; a network of zig-zagging trenches burrowed out of the battle-scarred earth that ran away to the south, following the contours of the undulating terrain and congesting around the burned ruins of a nearby village. Then the enemy's anti-tank and anti-aircraft positions came into sight, revealed as dark sandbagged clumps on the landscape concealed under tarpaulins and camouflage nets.

Elway turned his head slowly east, his view foreshortening. He could see the shimmering silver thread of the Oder River and several ruined pontoon bridges. Further away to the southwest was a black tortured scar of ground where the remains of Schwedt stood, the buildings there still smouldering smoke into the sky.

The dawn came on but the smoke muted the light so there were no shadows, and nothing to give Elway's eyes perspective. Distances were distorted and the dull light softened the edges of everything, making the battlefield appear remote and blurred.

Then the first rays of sunrise spread their fingers across the landscape and the Russian tanks began to emerge.

They were a mix of T-90s and T-72s, Elway guessed. He could see a formation of parked vehicles far to the south in a shallow valley. The vehicles were too far away to identify and were positioned, he suspected, for an imminent push against Schwedt. Closer were two rows of T-72s parked along the western bank of the Oder. Some of the vehicles were draped with camouflage nets. Elway focused the binoculars and studied the enemy MBTs for a long moment, counting over thirty vehicles.

The sun poked through a bank of drifting smoke, aided by a chill nagging breeze. The haze was shredded and the sun's rays fell upon another formation of Russian tanks that were arrayed in a ragged line along a ridge just a few miles to the southwest. The Russian tanks were dug in and bristled on the crest of the rise like a barbed-wire line. Elway pointed to the tanks and then the mud-furrowed tracks that suggested the vehicles had covertly moved into position during the night.

"T-90s," he said darkly. "Maybe as many as thirty of them. They're behind earthworks along that ridge. There's no way our intel would know about them. They're right across the line of advance of the Abrams'. Our tanks are going to run headlong into them in less than thirty minutes and they'll be cut to pieces."

Wolf snatched for the binoculars and peered hard. Then he swung his attention to the western skyline. He could see the approaching dust cloud of the Abrams tanks speeding towards disaster. They were coming on fast, tiny specks in the lenses of the binoculars, but growing as the vehicles bounced and jolted over the ground.

"Surely they must know the Russians are waiting for them…" Elway said uneasily. He scanned the smoke-thick sky, expecting to see a wave of Apache helicopters suddenly appear ahead of the column. His elation at the sight of the advancing allied tanks began to turn to trepidation and then became a queasy sense of sickening foreboding. He glanced uneasily to the south and made a closer inspection of the enemy's other positions. Now he could see movement in the trenches, suggesting a Russian alert was scrambling men to their ready positions – although whether it was in response to news of the imminent Allied tank attack, or whether the Russians were merely emerging from a brief few hours of rest was uncertain. Those trenches would be bristling with RPGs.

And still the Abrams tanks came on, gathering speed and spreading out, their formations beginning to fragment as some tanks pulled ahead and others were disrupted by terrain undulations and shell craters.

"It's going to be a fucking slaughter!" Elway gasped. He turned in a slow despairing circle and was suddenly struck by the horrific understanding of just how vulnerable they were; unsupported and two kilometers behind the Russian positions.

"Holy Mary, mother of God," he gasped. Until this moment the stark appreciation of their perilous position had been concealed by the cloak of night. Now the realization struck him with a savage jolt.

"We've got to do something!" Karl Wolf watched the Abrams tanks draw inexorably closer. He threw down the binoculars and ran towards the center of town in a desperate race against time.

*

Karl Wolf charged up the rear ramp of his command vehicle and leaped for the radio. He fired off a frantic message to his Battalion HQ, warning that the Allied armored attack was charging towards annihilation. Then he dashed back to where Elway stood. The American was peering at the advance of the tanks with macabre ghoulish compulsion. It was like he was a bystander witnessing a tragic car crash in slow motion as it unravelled before his eyes.

"They're not turning!" Wolf said with despair. He no longer needed the binoculars. The advancing line of Abrams tanks were only about seven kilometers away. The MBTs were cresting a gentle rise; their great steel tracks churning the earth into a trailing plume of mud and dust.

And still the Abrams came on.

"Christ!" Elway stared in appalled disbelief. He turned the binoculars on to the waiting line of T-90s and saw sudden scatters of movement. Men were scrambling aboard their tanks, emerging from a nest of drab grey tents. Engines roared into life, spewing dark clouds of diesel exhaust.

"Jesus Christ!" Wolf gaped. "Why aren't our tanks slowing or turning?"

The sound of the Abrams' charging was a low earth trembling rumble; a sound that quivered the air and echoed off the clouds.

"The Russians know something is up!" Elway pointed. He saw one of the Russian tank's turret turn. Behind the line of vehicles several Russian officers were running through the mud, moving between the tanks and barking instructions to each commander.

"My God!" Elway mouthed. "The Abrams' must almost be within long range."

Karl Wolf turned on his heel and sprinted back into the town. When he returned just sixty seconds later, he was being trailed by four Bundeswehr soldiers, carrying between them two of the MILAN firing posts and several missiles.

"We have to warn the Abrams'!" Wolf said in a rush, ordering the men to set the anti-tank systems up in the long grass.

Elway watched on. "What are you planning to do?"

"We're going to fire at the T-90s," Wolf declared.

"You'll reveal our position to the enemy. Within ten minutes the road up the slope of this hill will be crawling with fucking Russians," Elway said.

"I know," Wolf's voice was calm; resigned. "But if we do nothing the entire allied armored attack will be destroyed."

The two MILAN teams worked with the dextrous skill of men who were well-drilled. The gunners placed the weapon system's sight markers on the base of the two closest Russian tanks, then looked to their officer for confirmation.

"Fire!"

The first gunner pressed the firing button.

The loaded missile launched from its container and the tube ejected out the rear of the launcher. The instant the missile was activated stabilizing fins deployed and then the sustainer rocket ignited with a loud *'whoosh!'*.

The missile streaked across the battlefield.

The MILAN was a wire-guided SACLOS (semi-automatic command to line-of-sight) weapon. The gunner remained hunched over the controls as the missile flashed towards its target. Wolf held his breath.

The range was just over two thousand yards, and the flight time took several seconds. But even before the missile struck, Wolf saw with sudden despair that the little speck of bright light in the distance was dipping and veering. A second later the missile exploded, missing the target enemy tank and erupting an avalanche of earthworks that protected the MBT on three sides.

"Reload!"

The second gunner launched his missile and again a bright darting speck of light went streaking across the sky. Elway and Wolf exchanged glances. "You've just signed our death warrants," Elway said matter-of-factly.

"Yes," Karl Wolf conceded.

The second MILAN missile flew straight as an arrow, steered unerringly towards its unsuspecting target. The missile struck the T-90 in the vehicle's thinly armored rear and the tank erupted in a billowing fireball of bright orange flame and a rolling cloud of black smoke. The sound of the sudden explosion clapped wickedly against the sky.

Wolf flicked his eyes from the burning fireball to the advancing American tanks and saw, with relief, the lead vehicles stop abruptly and then begin to disperse and dramatically alter course. Three of the Abrams popped off smoke grenades and Wolf's view quickly became obscured.

For a full ninety seconds the battlefield remained eerily mute – and then everything seemed to happen at once.

Four American Apache AH-64D helicopters came swooping from out of the west. Flying low to the ground, they appeared through the drifting smoke as dark menacing misshapen specs. They flashed over the Russian positions with their ASE (Aircraft Survivability Equipment) suites turned on. The ASE gear was the first thing the Apache pilots had activated, well before they reached the Russian lines. The gear was high-tech wizardry designed to give the crews aboard the helicopters the very best chance of survival and included a jammer, CMWS (Common Missile Warning System), AVR-2 laser detectors and APR-39 radar warning receivers.

The Apaches targeted the Russian T-90s arrayed hull-down along the ridge, unleashing AGM-114R Hellfire missiles from the firing rails attached to pylons mounted to their wings. The Romeo missiles were the current standard Apache loadout and incorporated a dual warhead that was designed, first to defeat reactive armor, and second to defeat turret armor.

The attack was choreographed like a deadly dance by the CPG (co-pilot, gunner) in the lead helicopter which had been fitted with the AN/APG-78 Longbow radar. The CPG identified targets and relayed the information to the other three birds in the flight. A fusillade of missiles streaked away on wicked flashing tails of grey smoke.

The air above the battlefield became criss-crossed with arcs of smoke and fire. The Russian infantry who were hunkered down in nearby trenches fired 9K34 Strela-3 (SA-14 Gremlin) MANPADS. One of the Apaches was targeted and the helicopter's automated systems activated immediately as the onboard CMWS optical sensors detected the UV spike from the launch. The helicopter automatically began spitting flares from the four flare buckets on the tailboom. The Strela-3 locked on to the Apache and zeroed in. The pilot tried vainly to avoid the incoming enemy missile, throwing his helo across the smoke-stained sky, gritting his teeth and fighting with the controls while all around him warning alarms flashed and wailed. The pilot's frantic efforts to evade the missile were to no avail. The missile streaked past the stricken helicopter and cleaved off the tail rotor assembly. The Apache fell from the sky like a stone and crashed into a furrowed muddy field. Another Apache went spiraling out of control, turning crazily below its thrashing rotors, trailing a great plume of black billowing smoke. Turbines screaming, the helicopter ploughed nose-first into a mound of mud-churned ground and erupted in flames.

The remaining two Apaches unleashed the last of their Hellfire missiles on the Russian T-90s and then turned their vengeful fury on the ragged line of Russian infantry trenches, firing their 30mm M230 chain guns. The brutal cannon was slaved to the pilots' helmet sights and the trenches were an unmissable ugly scar scraped across the fields below them. A storm of rounds churned the muddy trench line onto a charnel house of blood and gore. The chain guns roared for just a few brief seconds but the devastation wrecked upon the Russian lines was apocalyptic. Then the two surviving birds pirouetted in the sky and fled westwards, gaining height and the cover of drifting smoke as they retreated.

In the aftermath of the attack, six Russian T-90s had been reduced to burning ruin, the smoke clouds from their mangled wreckage smearing a dark smudge of haze across the battlefield.

Wolf turned away from the scene, grimly satisfied. He met the look in Elway's eyes with level frankness. "We have alerted the advancing tanks. Now there is nothing more we can do to help the attack. We must instead look to our own survival."

"You've put a target on our backs," Elway said. "The Russians are going to come for us. They can't allow us to remain here behind their lines. They're going to send everything they've got against us."

"Yes," Wolf admitted, then pointed southeast towards the banks of the Oder River where a column of Russian IFVs was winding its way towards the town. "It's already happening…"

*

Elway had just one priority as he ran back towards the center of town, shouting the alarm as he pounded along the main street. "Bravo Company to me! Bravo Company to me!"

He reached the eastern outskirts and stared, following the road down the steep slope to where it ended abruptly at the destroyed bridge over the Oder. Russian IFVs were trundling towards the ruined bridge, apparently planning to intersect the road and use it for an assault up the hill.

Elway looked at the dozen or so survivors of Bravo Company that had gathered around him. Sergeant Moon had a pair of binoculars pressed to his eyes.

"They're BMP-2s," Moon said.

"And they'll be crammed full of mechanized infantry," Elway was certain. "We've got to barricade the road right here and then relocate the remaining Panzerfausts and MILANs. I want everything we can find, stacked right here. Furniture, rubble – anything that might slow the bastards up for a few seconds."

The Americans scattered, kicking down nearby doors and dragging sofas, chairs and tables onto the road. The rest of the street was already prepared, and men were already in fortified positions – but up until this moment the eastern approach to the town could not be blocked for fear the Russians might have noticed and realized the site had been seized by the allies. Now there was no more need for discretion. The Russians were coming and all hell was about to break loose.

"Move your asses!" Elway snapped and chivvied, his voice cracking like a whip. A handful of Bundeswehr soldiers abandoned their posts to join the frantic scramble. Any barricade short of concrete Jersey barriers were unlikely to slow the enemy armored personnel carriers for long – but just a few seconds of hesitation from the Russian drivers was all a good operator on a Panzerfaust or a MILAN needed to take a killing shot. And once the first enemy vehicles were disabled, the rest of the troop carriers would be blocked from entering the town.

When Kurt Wolf arrived at the outskirts, Elway drew him aside, his face dripping with sweat and his features working with agitation.

"We have to hit the bastards as soon as they leave the fields and start climbing the road," Elway said. "Every one of those vehicles will be jammed full of mech infantry. If they're allowed to reach the crest and disgorge their men, we'll be overwhelmed. We have to kill the bastards while they're still in their vehicles."

"Agreed," Wolf saw the tactical situation in an instant. "I'll reposition the MILANS, but the Panzerfausts remain where they are – just in case the plan doesn't work."

"Fair enough," Elway agreed.

There were four MILANs dispersed in the houses and on street corners throughout the town. Wolf ordered them all brought forward and into positions from where they could fire down into the advancing column of enemy IFVs.

A sudden roar of jet engines overhead caught Elway by surprise. For one dreadful instant he thought that the Russians had ordered Su-25 'Frogfoots' to attack the town, but when he scanned the eastern skyline, he saw none of the menacing shapes approaching. Instead, the sound was coming from high overhead. Elway craned his neck and through the scrims of grey smoke saw Allied and Russian fighter jets engaged in a high-altitude dog-fight. He could not identify the aircraft as they flashed and swerved and echoed across the sky, but he saw the jets exchange missiles and then the Russian fighter suddenly became erratic, jinking and pulling tight G-turns as a missile hunted him across the blue vastness. A few seconds later the sky lit with a bright bloom of flame and two seconds after that the echo of the explosion reverberated. The enemy fighter fell from the sky in a thousand burning pieces and the Allied fighter turned south. Elway assumed the Allied armored attack was advancing under air cover and that gave him an idea. He went in search of Kurt Wolf and found the German officer weighed down with reload missiles for a MILAN.

"You need to get on the radio to Allied Command and let them know we hold the town," Elway insisted.

"I already have," Wolf said. "I have informed Battalion –"

"Then tell them again," Elway insisted. "NATO Command needs to know we're here and that we need air support," he thrust a finger into the sky. "Those are Allied fighters. They're obviously providing air support to the armored advance. We need to call for CAS (close air support). There must be an AWACS circling somewhere behind the battlefront. If we can be patched through to a JTAC (Joint Terminal Attack Controller) they can put out an 'All Players' call to one of the fighters."

Wolf nodded. "You do it," he said. "My command Marder is hull down in the ruins of the bakery. Tell the operator what we need, American, and then pray someone is listening to us, eh?" The German sounded bizarrely buoyant and it unnerved Elway. Wolf seemed utterly immune to the tension and the looming danger. Now the Krasukhas had been destroyed and the approaching Abrams warned that they were charging headlong into a trap, the Bundeswehr officer seemed to be almost relishing the prospect of a savage fight in the town's ruins. Elway decided the German was either resigned to death, or an actor worthy of Hollywood. Elway didn't show the same calm composure. He sprinted towards the bakery as fast as he could, his big arms pumping and his leaden, weary legs turning rubbery from exhaustion; running as if his life depended on it.

Because it probably did.

*

There were twelve Russian BMP-2s in the column. The lead vehicle set itself to the eastern approach to Kleine Grenzstadt and the rest of the column followed, snaking their way higher, slowing each time the road switched back during its ascent and then accelerating again once each bend had been negotiated. The column compressed and then extended like a concertina as it trundled up the steep incline.

Karl Wolf watched the vehicles from the window of a building on the outskirts of the town and urged himself to patience. The first MILAN missiles needed to be killing shots. This was the one chance he had to land a serious blow against the enemy before the battle broke down into confusion, flames and ragged firefights. He could hear the growling engines of the enemy vehicles, revving in low gear as the incline slowed them and then he was standing in the middle of the road behind the makeshift barricade.

He glanced left and right. There were two MILANs set up on opposite sides of the road behind sandbagged emplacements, and a third one in the second story window of a nearby building.

Wolf waited. He watched the two-man crews behind the sandbags checking and re-checking the range to the enemy BMPs and Wolf did not hurry them. He wanted the operators to be calm and concentrated. Chivvying them to hasty action would only unsettle them. The first few seconds of the battle were critical, Wolf understood. One well-aimed blow would stun the Russians and seize the initiative; everything hinged on that first salvo of anti-tank missiles.

"Are you ready?" Wolf kept his tone of voice conversational, as though there wasn't a convoy of armored enemy fighting vehicles storming up the rise and now just five hundred meters from where he stood. He deliberately restrained himself from staring at the approaching enemy vehicles. He wanted to portray an image of casual composure.

Hank Elway spoiled the moment. The American came running down the middle of the road, breathing hard and swaying on his feet from numbing exhaustion. "The Russians are jamming comms," he said between ragged gulps of breath. "I can't reach command to call in air support. The enemy must have other EWS in the area – either on the ground or in the air behind the lines. I'm getting nothing but fucking static."

Wolf took the news with a grimace of pain which he quickly camouflaged. "Very well. Then we have no other option but to fight the Russians ourselves."

The German turned his attention back to the MILANs and then, despite himself, he glanced through the barricade at the approaching BMP-2s.

Christ! They were close!

Wolf figured the range to be just a few hundred yards. He saw the MILAN teams were hunched over their weapons, poised.

"Fire!"

The two MILANs on either side of the road fired first, and after a heartbeat of delay, the MILAN in the second story window fired. All three anti-tank missiles flew from their launchers trailing their shimmering guidance wires and streaked down the slope. The lead Russian IFV took two direct hits. Both missiles slammed into the BMP-2's sloped frontal hull armor and exploded. The devastating impact as the twin collisions erupted blew the Russian IFV into a million small fragments of twisted metal, killing the crew and every soldier aboard in a searing flash of white-hot light and a cascade of black smoke. The retort of the explosions cracked against the sky like a bullwhip and rumbled amongst the clouds.

The MILAN fired from the building's window targeted the second vehicle in the column and struck it broadside just as the BMP was accelerating out of a bend. The missile struck the vehicle's thin hull armor directly below the low-profile conical turret. The warhead detonated on impact, tearing a gaping hole in the steel plating and a moment later the Russian vehicle crashed to a halt and burst into flames. The screams of the soldiers trapped inside the burning vehicle were gruesome shrieks of terror. The nerve-shredding sounds as they burned alive carried up the hill to where Wolf and Elway stood.

Neither man spoke. Instead, they watched the rest of the infantry fighting vehicles slam to a halt and a few seconds later the rear doors of the BMP-2s flew open and armed soldiers burst into the open.

"Fire!" Hank Elway cried.

The dozen surviving Americans were in buildings around the eastern outskirts of the town. A SAW opened up on the Russian infantry, cutting down a handful of men as they dashed for the long grass and rocks beside the road. One of the Russians was hit in the thigh and fell to the blacktop, wriggling and screaming as bright red blood spilled across the asphalt. The soldier beside the wounded man opened his mouth to shout an order, but he was flung backwards, sent reeling as though he had been punched by an almighty fist, his helmet spinning from his head and his assault rifle clattering to the ground. The man collapsed and his corpse fell on top of the soldier with a bullet lodged in his thigh.

Elway carried his M4 to the barricade and opened fire. Around him other small arms added their thunder to the chaos. The Russians were trapped in the open and the Americans were combat veterans, well trained and ruthless. Their apprehension was gone now; the anxiety throughout the hours of waiting and preparation for this moment when they could unleash their own small hell upon the enemy. Elway felt a fierce exhilaration as the M4 at his shoulder swung and fired, swung and then fired again.

Sweat dribbled down his face from beneath the rim of his helmet and clung in his eyebrows and stung his eyes. Shards of dust and dirt hung in the air and choked him. The smoke from the burning Russian vehicles crawled up the face of the slope and drifted through the street.

A handful of Russians fought back.

The vehicles at the rear of the column reversed to clear their lines of fire and the autocannons atop their turrets erupted spitting flames. Something clanged against Elway's helmet, the impact fierce enough to jerk his head back on his shoulders. He ducked down behind cover, his ears ringing. He felt the side of his face for blood but found none, but for a long moment his senses swam, and his eyes were unfocussed. All around him he could hear the roar of battle but the sound came to him muted and muffled. He reloaded his weapon and opened fire again. Sergeant Moon appeared from the far side of the street; his face scowled with concern.

"You okay, sir?"

"Yeah."

"Your head?"

Elway pressed his hand to his helmet and his fingers found a deep dent. "I'm okay."

Moon looked amazed. "You just got hit with a chunk of fuckin' metal the size of a house brick. You sure you're okay?"

"Yes," Elway said, then, as if to prove the point, he thrust the barrel of his M4 through a chink in the makeshift barricade and shot a Russian soldier, hitting the man in the buttocks as he scrambled across Elway's line of sight. The Russian went down in the long grass, clutching at his wound.

Kurt Wolf now sensed the fight could be won on the town's outskirts. The Russian attack had stalled and the mechanized infantry that spilled from the IFVs were being ruthlessly cut down by the Americans. He ordered two squads of his men to abandon their positions along the street and called them forward to the barricade.

"Show no mercy to the enemy!" Wolf urged his men as they added their firepower to the fury the Americans were unleashing. "They invade our land! They destroy our towns! They rape and murder our women and children! Kill them all!"

The two MILANs behind sandbags on the curbside fired again. Another Russian BMP disappeared in a black pall of smoke. The second missile clipped the turret of a vehicle and whanged away into the distance. The German gunner swore bitterly and barked for a reload, then screamed in agony as Russian autocannon fire hammered the position. Both the gunner and his loader were hit. The loader was shot in the back and the 30mm shell punched a hole the size of a fist through his torso, killing him instantly. The gunner died from gruesome head wounds.

Wolf and Elway ducked as more autocannon fire flayed the barricade and the walls of the surrounding houses. Two of the

BMPs were attempting to charge up the rise, shouldering the destroyed and burning vehicles ahead of them off the road. As they advanced and continued to fire, both Russian vehicles popped off 81mm smoke grenades from the projectors mounted on their turrets.

But for the mechanized infantry laying in soft cover amidst the long grass and rocks by the side of the road, the attack by the two defiant IFVs was not the opportunity to charge they had been waiting for. Instead, the dismounted Russian troops began to retreat down the slope, using the dense grey smoke screen to conceal their withdrawal.

Elway realized the two IFVs approaching the barricade were isolated and were moving forward without essential infantry support. He could see the BMPs clearly as they loomed like prehistoric monsters out of the white-grey mist. He shot a glance sideways expecting to see the MILAN team behind their sandbags lining up a close-range shot, but the emplacement was empty.

"Christ!"

At the last possible instant, Sergeant Moon seized Elway by the collar and flung him bodily to the sidewalk. A heartbeat later the first BMP-2 crashed through the barricade, the front of the huge mechanical beast rearing up over the jumble of furniture and then slamming down again like an avalanche of steel. Elway and Moon scrambled to safety as the two BMPs barged through the barricade, scattering debris and junk aside, their turrets turning and their autocannons blazing away at the windows of the surrounding buildings.

Then, from several hundred yards further along the street, a flicker of light and a puff of grey smoke appeared from the window of a distant building. A Panzerfaust projectile flew like a dart and struck the lead BMP high up on the vehicle's front hull. The explosion as the warhead detonated rumbled through the ground like an earthquake and the Russian IFV dissolved into thousands of jagged steel fragments and a blot of black smoke. Flames leaped from the twisted wreckage. The rear doors of the IFV were sprung open by the hammer blow force of the explosion. When Elway peered inside, he saw a sickening pulp of burning bloody gore, the inhabitants so mutilated, so disfigured, that they were no longer recognizable as human.

The second BMP-2 driver turned his vehicle and plowed through the front wall of a small café. Glass shattered and the façade collapsed as the troop carrier mounted the curb and crashed forward. But without sufficient momentum, the Russian vehicle slowed, then stalled, wedged sideways in the debris of concrete and brick walls.

The German Panzerfaust operator couldn't miss. The rear doors of the BMP-2 were flung open as the troops inside tried to scramble to safety, realizing the imminent danger. The vehicle's turret turned, but it was wedged in a tangle of shattered wooden beams. The Panzerfaust operator took a heartbeat longer than necessary to be sure of the shot and then fired the weapon. The projectile streaked through the air and struck the BMP-2, punching clean through the thin hull armor and exploding the troop-carrying compartment to pieces. Every man aboard was killed in a blinding flash of fire. The percussive force of the explosion knocked Elway off his feet. He landed hard on the sidewalk and then rolled to his left as twisted steel fell from the sky, crashing down along the street. The heat from the explosion washed over Elway in a searing wave. By the time he had scrambled to his knees, flames were devouring the destroyed vehicle and the air filled with choking clouds of oily smoke.

In the aftermath of the explosion followed an eerie brittle silence. Slowly, the German and American soldiers emerged from their firing positions and gathered in the town's main street with a sense of incredulous disbelief. They had held off the first determined enemy attack, but at the cost of several dead and wounded.

Wolf and Elway went forward, clambering over the ruins of the barricade to stand by the roadside. The Russian column was a jumble of gutted vehicles and a scatter of dead bodies. In the long grass, the enemy's wounded were trying to make their way back down the slope, some dragging shattered legs behind them, one man clutching his guts, another staggering, his face a mask of blood.

Wolf let them go – not out of compassion, but simply to conserve ammunition.

"Next time will be harder," Elway said darkly.

"Next time they will use artillery and rockets before they launch an assault," Wolf opined.

The layers of smoke between the town and the bank of the Oder were so thick that for several moments there was nothing either man could see of the enemy's next assault. Then suddenly the curtain of haze to the north of the steep hill was torn apart and through the black smoke emerged a phalanx of tanks, surging across the war-torn ground at high speed.

For a split-second Hank Elway froze with dread and despair. Then he gaped, his eyes wide with the sudden wonder of relief. The tanks were mud-spattered Abrams M1A2s that had encircled the enemy's lines and were now charging along the western bank of the river like a pack of ravenous wolves amongst an unsuspecting flock of chickens.

"They're ours!" Elway whooped and his face lit with relief.

Even Kurt Wolf's dispassionate, dour expression dissolved into a rare smile. "Thank God," he murmured and drew a deep shuddering breath. "Thank God."

For now, at least, the fight for the town was over.

The tank battle in the fields to the north and south was just beginning.

Chapter 10:

The commander of the Abrams Battalion was a wily old fox who had spent his entire military career in the tank corps. As soon as he realized he was charging towards a dug-in line of enemy MBTs, he halted the advance and ordered a handful of his tanks to pop smoke. Now, he had a problem.

Lieutenant Colonel Matt Zimmermann's orders called for him to crash through the Russian flank and drive an armored wedge between the enemy's lines for the German Leopards advancing further to his north to exploit. But the notion of a frontal assault against hull-down T-90s was akin to a suicide mission.

Instead, he ordered two Companies of his Abrams north to circumnavigate the hilltop town of Kleine Grenzstadt and encircle the Russian positions. The T-90s had wedded themselves to their crest and their hull-down earthworks. Therefore, Zimmermann would make them pay by catching them in the flank and crushing them between a hammer and an anvil.

Twenty-eight Abrams M1A2s broke from the main body of the Battalion and raced northwards behind a blinding veil of smoke while the remaining Abrams under Zimmermann's command crept closer to the ridge until they were able to engage the enemy at long range. The American Colonel had no illusions; a duel fought at ranges close to four kilometers was unlikely to cause either tank force damage; both the American Abrams and the Russian T-90s were too thoroughly armored to be destroyed from over a thousand meters – but that wasn't the point.

Now the Russians knew the American tanks were approaching, Zimmermann had to give the enemy something to fire at – something to hold their attention while the encircling tanks swept around behind them.

*

The two Companies of Abrams tanks sent to circumnavigate Kleine Grenzstadt moved out in echelon, obscured from the enemy's view by billowing smoke and then the vast monolith of rock upon which the town was perched. The tanks advanced at high speed and each commander pre-loaded with sabot rounds while the vehicles were on the move. The crews took a few last deep breaths to settle jangling nerves. They shared the tense banter and small-talk of men about to face danger. The Abrams were mud-spattered and had been streaked with grime during the long journey from the harbors of northern Germany. The air inside the tanks was ripe with the stench of body odor; the smell of nervous sweat suffocating and sour.

Orders from command vehicles crackled and hissed intermittently into headsets. One by one the Abrams re-orientated until they were formed into the shape of a vast wedge with the lead tanks at the steel tip of the formation and the echelons spreading a kilometer wide on either flank.

They were fresh tanks; a newly arrived Battalion to the battle for Europe, but the crews were well-trained and many were veterans who had seen combat action in the Middle East. The crewmen aboard were eager to prove themselves in the cauldron of fire; keen to do their duty and serve the cause of freedom. The sight of the American tanks surging through the scrims of grey smoke as they charged to battle was gloriously stirring... and terrifying.

Some crewmen fidgeted nervously, waiting to be called into action, clinging to a hand-hold while the tanks jounced and swayed and reared over the muddy ground. A driver reached for the lucky rabbit's foot he wore around his neck. Loaders rehearsed their actions, going over in their minds the intricate moves required to feed a fresh round into the gun breech. Some men yawned involuntarily. Every man was pumped full of adrenaline and trembling with anxious fear.

The forward tanks rounded the foot of the steep rocky rise and steered south at last. Two kilometers to their left was the slate grey waters of the Oder River. Ahead of them, spread out in ragged milling disorder, was the flank of the Russian line. Through the drifts of smoke trucks and artillery pieces appeared. The trucks were parked by the riverbank in great immobile phalanxes and across the Oder were several new pontoon bridges in the midst of construction. Then the advancing Abrams came upon a parked column of BMP-1s and thousands of infantry. The troops were camped on the banks of the river, some in muddy tents but most in shallow trenches that had not been dug as fortifications, but merely to shelter the men from surprise NATO air attacks. The men and machines and guns were part of the Russian force massing to strike west to outflank the Allies – and the American tanks burst through the smoke and into a killer's playground, taking the enemy completely by surprise.

The Abrams accelerated, the vehicles pitching and heaving over the uneven ground. Vehicle commanders peered at their CITV screens and were overwhelmed with targets.

"Engage! Engage!" each tank's comms system erupted with a static hiss of orders.

The formation became ragged as some tanks veered to close on Russian APCs and the air filled with the chaotic swirl of screams and explosions and billowing black smoke.

There was no time for caution or to consider consequences. Pumped full of adrenaline and with their CITV screens cluttered with soft enemy targets, the Abrams charged into the melee, battle lust fizzing in the crews' blood and their eyes misted red with the warrior's rage.

Ahead of the tanks, the Russian BMPs were lined up like targets on a firing range and beyond the troop carriers were helpless infantry and trucks. There was nothing the BMPs could do to slow the American tanks. They were fifty-year-old relics of the Soviet era, shipped to the battlefront to serve as troop transports that would speed the Russian infantry west once the enemy attack had commenced. Their 73mm 2A28 Grom main guns were no match for the well-armored Abrams but despite that fact a few alert crews managed to fire on the attacking Americans. Two of the Russian APC crews launched

'Fagot' (AT-4 Spigot) missiles, but neither missile hit its target. The 'Fagot' was a wire-guided Semi-automatic Command to Line of Sight (SACLOS) missile, vaguely similar to the MILAN used by the Allies. The weapon had a hit probability of around eighty-percent, provided the operator continued to keep the weapon's crosshair on the target in order to guide the missile. The missiles launched and streaked across the battlefield, their red tail-lights bright against the grey sullen sky, but the two BMPs came under immediate fire from several Abrams tanks and were immolated in huge fireballs of flame. The 'Fagot' missiles, no longer guided, speared off into the black smoke.

The firefight raged for just a few short seconds, the tanks pirouetting and spinning in the churned mud, picking off the defenseless Russian troop carriers at will. Outgunned and static, the BMP-1s were obliterated as the American tanks fired their pre-loaded sabot rounds, then reloaded with AMP (Advanced Multi-Purpose) rounds and fired again. The comms network aboard the Abrams became overloaded with chatter – voices competing with each other in the bloody chaos. One Abrams inadvertently charged into a deep ditch and became bogged, its nose buried in the ground and its tracks unable to gain purchase in the glutinous mud. Two Abrams collided when one of the vehicles T-boned the other in the swirling smoke. One of the vehicles lost its track and was stranded in the mire, but the rest of the Abrams surged on, flowing around the burning destroyed wreckage of the ravaged BMPs and setting their sights on the columns of trucks and milling infantry in the distance.

Some of the trucks began to move, belching huge clouds of dirty diesel exhaust as they tried to escape the approaching storm of fiery death. The infantry scrambled from their tents like ants from an overturned nest. Some men turned and fled towards the pontoon bridges across the Oder. A few men reached for RPG-7s, but most simply stood rooted to the spot in shock and awe as the earth beneath their feet rumbled and shuddered and the shrieking whine of the Abrams turbines sounded like the blood-curdling scream of banshees.

The Abrams crashed through the column of trucks and into the flank of the Russians. Mud churned from the steel tank tracks was flung high to mist the air, and the sounds of the battlefield turned to screams of agony punched through by the wicked crack of the Abrams guns and the hammering chatter of their coax machine guns. The trucks and troops were soft targets. The loaders in each tank's turret were lathered in sweat from serving their guns. Now the Abrams powerful machine guns were unleashed, shredding the parked trucks and flailing the maze of narrow trenches with a withering hail of crossfire.

The Abrams had lost all cohesion in the milling madness of the fight, but still they crashed home like some monstrous battering ram, punching great holes in the Russian line, collapsing the shallow trenches under their seventy-tons of steel weight and their massive churning tracks. Some Russians were crushed and ground into the mud. Others abandoned their scant cover and fled south, blundering through the mire, their faces white with stricken terror. More men vainly fled towards the riverbank, but the pontoon bridges were still incomplete. Some Russian troops milled in pathetic terror on the muddy bank. Others threw themselves into the brown silted water and tried to swim to safety. They were trapped like rats on a sinking ship, cowering in terror as the Abrams turret-mounted coax machine guns hunted them mercilessly. A truck was torn to pieces by a flail of heavy machine gun fire and exploded in a spectacular bloom of flames and smoke. The truck beside it was consumed by the spreading fireball. A furnace-like wave of heat washed over the battlefield and then the sky turned black with oily smoke. Two more trucks exploded. Another was punched full of holes but merely sagged on its shredded tires, offering temporary cover to a handful of Russians. The Abrams commander who had fired on the truck ordered his driver to accelerate. The Abrams speared into the damaged truck and reared up, then crashed down like an executioner's axe, crushing the vehicle and killing the men who had been cowering behind its chassis.

The battle became a merciless slaughter and the Americans slaked themselves; drenched themselves in the enemy's blood.

A battery of four Russian 152mm 2A65 Msta-B howitzers were destroyed by the advancing Abrams with AMP rounds. The enemy artillery pieces were hooked up to their KrAZ-260 6x6 trucks and stood parked in a column on the western bank of the Oder. The guns were destroyed, and the hapless crews scrambled from the trucks as machine gun fire shredded the vehicles. The crewmen floundered in the mire, running for their lives – but there was no safe haven. Bullets cut them down and then the tanks rolled on.

The stench of blood and guts and smoke and oil hung over the battlefield. Wounded Russian infantry writhed in the filth and their blood soaked the ground. Some men died instantly. Others lingered, their bodies torn to pieces, their screams of agony shrill and piercing. One brave Russian fired an RPG from a narrow shallow trench. The projectile slammed into the turret of an Abrams, scorching the armored metal but doing no other damage. For his defiance, the man's reward was a vengeful burst of machine gun fire that tore his body apart as if it had been thrown under a butcher's axe.

Having decimated the BMPs and slaughtered the Russian infantry, the American tanks continued their sweep south, turning to take the line of Russian T-90 MBTs in the rear.

The Abrams left a gruesome trail of carnage and chaos in their wake and plunged gallantly towards the waiting barricade of Russian tanks. The attack had been fragmented and scattered by the melee amongst the enemy's troop carriers, trucks and infantry so that the American tanks surged forward in clusters, scattered across the mud-churned landscape.

A makeshift service road loomed ahead, cutting through the terrain parallel to the American tanks. It had evidently been bulldozed out of the lush fields to provide ease of movement behind the enemy's lines. The first Abrams reached the mud-rutted trail and suddenly came under fire from further to the south where a Battalion of T-72s were stationed. Alerted to the Allied flank attack, the Russians were scrambling to fight back.

The T-72s were on the move, not in formation, but merely flinging themselves frantically into the fray while ahead of the Abrams the first of the enemy T-90s were reversing from their earthworks and trying to turn to face the looming onslaught.

The Americans were suddenly caught in a hail of panicked fire. The T-72s presented the most immediate danger for the Abrams were broadside to their 125mm D-81 Smoothbore guns.

The T-72 was the mainstay of the Russian army and had been in service since the early 1970s. Over fifty thousand T-72s had been built, and at that moment, on those muddy fields of eastern Germany, it seemed to the American Abrams commanders that all fifty thousand of the god-damned beasts were firing at them. Russian sabot rounds slashed through the air and suddenly the ground around the American tankers was upheaved in explosions and fireballs of flames so that it seemed as if the earth were splitting open in a vast volcanic eruption. One Abrams took a direct hit on the turret from two thousand yards. The enemy sabot round clanged off the composite Chobham armor with the sound of a tolling bell. The Abrams emerged through the smoke intact, but with sensitive electronic equipment damaged. Another Abrams lost its front left track to a round fired by a T-72. The sabot round smashed into the tank's rear road gear and the vehicle slewed to a drunken halt in the boggy mud.

The ragged line of Abrams were sheeted in mud and grime. Their turrets turned towards the T-72s and they fired on the move, still thundering across the shallow valley towards the T-90's that were now turning and preparing to meet the Americans head-on.

Aboard the Abrams the crews worked with a slavish dedication to their guns, driven by the discipline of their training. Orders were snapped, the words edged with rising anxiety and desperation. The initial bloodlust that had carried them this far into the snapping jaws of the enemy began to cool as the precarious peril of their situation showed through the billowing smoke. Some men silently quailed. Others went about their work with grim dedication. The exhilaration faded to be replaced with an ominous sense that they were hurtling towards the very gates of hell.

The Russian crews aboard the T-90s turned their turrets as the tanks pirouetted on their tracks to confront the Abrams. The Russian T-90 tanks main armament was the 2A46M-2 125mm smoothbore gun. Each tank's automatic loader carried twenty-two ready-to-fire rounds in its carousel. The commanders ordered sabot rounds fed into the breeches and eight seconds later the Russians were ready to fire and hunting targets amongst the closest American Abrams.

The Americans charged into a hail of fire, caught between the T-90s ahead of them and the T-72s to their south. One of the advancing Abrams was struck on the hull and stopped dead in the mud, the right side steel track blown to pieces and the tank's brush guard of reactive armor mangled, rendering the tank immobile. The disabled tank became an obstacle for the other Abrams to veer around. The T-90s fired again, this time at a range of just a thousand yards. Three Abrams took hits. Two emerged from the flash of flames and the great billow of black smoke undamaged but scorched. The third Abrams took a hit low on the front of its hull. The stunning impact of the explosion and a hail of shrapnel fragments damaged the tank's track. The vehicle spun sideways in the mud, temporarily veering out of control. Turned broadside to the dangerous T-90s, the Abrams was immediately vulnerable. On the ridge another T-90 fired on the Abrams.

The Russian tanks carried a loadout of 3BM60 Svinets-2 depleted uranium armor-piercing rounds. The round flashed from the barrel of the Russian tank trailing a thirty-foot long dragon's breath of fiery muzzle-flash.

The American crew inside the stranded Abrams did not see death coming. The Russian sabot round struck the tank broadside and the Svinets sabot round bored through the armor and exploded. The Abrams was torn apart from the inside and although the hull retained its integrity, the confined interior filled with a maelstrom of shrapnel fragments. The four-man crew were killed instantly, and the tank erupted in a billow of black smoke.

The leading Abrams plunged through wall of smoke, and when they emerged on the other side, they saw support crews for the T-90s scrambling into supply trucks and light utility vehicles. The coax machine guns in the turrets of the Abrams began their killing work. A Russian UAZ-469 burst into flames and veered sideways across the path of a fleeing 4x4 truck. The burning vehicle was crushed under the weight of the truck and both vehicles erupted in a fresh flare of flames and smoke. A KamAZ-5350 cargo truck was caught in a withering crossfire from two of the advancing Abrams and burst into flames. Another Abrams was forced to swerve sideways around a Russian truck that had careered into a ditch, but as the tank maneuvered, it made the fatal error of exposing its vulnerable side armor to the T-90s. Three shots rang out from the heights of the ridge, fired so close together that the sounds seemed to merge into one almighty thunderclap that rumbled like thunder through the clouds. The Abrams was hit in the rear and disabled. Its massive engine was turned to scrap metal and the vehicle began streaming a tail of oily smoke. The crew bailed out of the Abrams and scampered for cover in the mud-churned quagmire. Machine gun fire from a Russian tank cut the men down and killed them all.

Ignoring the less dangerous T-72s snapping at their flanks, the Abrams opened fire on the T-90s directly ahead of them. The range between the MBTs was closing by the minute. The first salvo of Abrams sabot rounds were fired from less than seven hundred yards. The effects were devastating.

The Americans had run the gauntlet of the Russian guns, stoically taking hits but driving forward regardless. Now they were in a knife-fight from lethally close range. Each Abrams already had a sabot round in the breech.

"Blue, Blue One. Engage at will!"

"Guidons, Apache Six. Continue the advance, get those slant reports up!"

One minute the crest of the far ridge was scattered with T-90s and the next moment the enemy MBTs were consumed by swirling smoke that enveloped the fields in a blanket of haze.

"Sabot up!" a tank's loader hollered to alert the gunner seated on the opposite side of the massive gun breech that there was already a sabot round loaded and ready for firing.

The tank's commander saw a T-90 emerge from a haze of smoke through his CITV and snapped the order. "Designate tank!" He thumbed a button on his commander's override handle causing the Abrams turret to automatically slew directly onto the target.

"Identified!" the gunner engaged the target and centered the sight reticle. He thumbed the laser button and a thin finger of light reached out for the target. Instantly the range flashed up on his display. The Abrams sophisticated fire control took over, plotting the distance to the target and lowering the barrel. It took the computer another split-second to calculate humidity and air density, and to measure the wind's speed and direction.

"Fire and adjust!" the commander gave the order. His voice was tight, his throat constricted with anxiety and intense pressure.

The gunner crushed the trigger. "On the way!"

The Abrams fired on the move, rocking back on its suspension as the sabot round left the barrel at the end of a thirty-foot muzzle blast.

The projectile flashed across the battlefield in the blink of an eye and hit the T-90 front on, striking the point on the enemy tank's hull where it joined to the turret. The impact was concealed behind a lurid flash of orange fire and a dense cloud of black smoke that funneled skyward. The sound of the direct hit rumbled across the sky, and when the boiling smoke finally dispersed, the T-90's turret had been unseated, the barrel pointing skyward and the hull billowing flames.

"Target!" the gunner declared with a growl of savage triumph. It was the Abrams tank crew's first kill of the campaign in Germany and somehow that split-second of brutal triumph changed the men. The uncertainty, the anxiety and the debilitating fear of failure melted away and was replaced with a calm sense of competence. They had been blooded in battle and emerged as warriors.

"Designate tank!" the killing continued.

*

Two American AAI RQ-7 Shadow UAVs circling high above the Oder River captured real time footage of the heroic Abrams charge and relayed the images via a C-band line-of-sight data link to the GCS (ground control station) several miles west of the fighting. From there the information was relayed to Lieutenant Colonel Zimmermann's command vehicle.

Zimmermann sensed the moment intuitively. The Russian T-90s had reversed from their emplacements and were turning to engage the two Companies of Abrams tanks storming into their rear. Now was the moment to close the range of the Russian tanks; to crush the T-90s in a close-range vice of firepower, and then to turn their collective force on the T-72's.

"Comanche Six, Mustang Six, advance on the ridge and engage!" the Colonel's voice crackled across the Battalion net.

The tanks of Comanche Company accelerated, eager to join the fray. With the Russian T-90s turned to fend off the attack at their rear, the Abrams surged forward and closed the range quickly. As they reached the ridge that the T-90s had been defending, the battlefield was spread out before them like a dramatic scene from an epic war film.

The T-90s were facing down the gentle reverse slope and bludgeoning their way towards them with the Oder River as a hazed backdrop, were the remains of the two Abrams Companies that had performed the outflanking maneuver. The Russian tanks were caught exactly where Colonel

Zimmermann had wanted them; squeezed between the iron jaws of a vice. Only the T-72s arriving from the south threatened the American pincer movement. Those tanks were closing on the flank of the Americans and were beginning to menace the momentum of the attack with accurate fire. Still more than a thousand yards away and therefore not an immediate lethal danger, the T-72s had the potential to throw back the attacking Abrams – if they could get close enough to target the thinner side and rear armor of the American tanks.

Colonel Zimmermann watched the battle unfold from his Command vehicle, his face tense and tight with frustration.

"Faster!" he urged Comanche Company on, muttering to himself, his voice edged with impatience. "Close on the fuckers and tear them to pieces." For Zimmermann, watching the battle via a bank of small relay monitors was excruciatingly frustrating. He wanted to be in the thick of the action. He wanted to be in direct control. No matter how high-tech the comms network and no matter how clear the images displayed on the screens before him, there was nothing that could replicate the savage reality of being in the midst of the battle. "Hit them!" he growled. "Don't let them seize the initiative!"

Zimmermann felt like an ex-champion footballer on the sideline of an NFL game, having retired from the sport and taken up coaching. He could scream from the sideline, and he could call the plays – but he couldn't quarterback the battle – and it was a torturous experience.

He barked a flurry of fresh orders across the Battalion net and then slumped back on the steel bench, gut-sick and powerless to do more.

The Abrams of Comanche Company opened fire on the T-90s from less than five hundred yards. Every tank in the Battalion was fitted with the US Army's FBCB2 Battle Management System, designed to reduce the fog of war by giving fighting units a digital display of all friendly forces. It also plotted the position of enemy units as they appeared. The image was superimposed on top of a map of the local terrain, displaying a two-mile square of ground. The BMSs aboard the tanks of Comanche Company lit up like a Christmas tree, displaying dozens of red enemy icons. Most were markers for the T-72s away to the south. The dozen or so red icons on the reverse slope of the ridge indicated the positions of the T-90s. But even though the battlefield was swirling with smoke and lit by the flames of burning tanks, the commanders aboard the closing Abrams didn't need electronic aids to identify their targets. The Russian MBTs were so close that the individual three-digit markings stenciled on their hulls and turrets were clearly identifiable. The T-90s were painted in single-colored camouflage dark green, but little of their paint scheme was visible through the spattered mud they wore.

"Engage at will!"

The fourteen tanks of Comanche Company opened fire from a range so close they could hardly miss. The Russian T-90s were decimated. In a single minute of fierce combat, every Russian tank that had been dug-in along the ridge was either destroyed or disabled. One T-90 was struck by two sabot rounds simultaneously. Both armor piercing projectiles crashed into the thin armored rear of the enemy tank. In a hundredth of a second the MBT was obliterated, disappearing in a blinding double-flash of fire. The tank blew up and outwards, flinging twisted chunks of scorched smoking metal into the sky. The explosions rang like thunderclaps across the clouds.

Two T-90s were disabled. Both of the enemy tanks took broadside hits to their hulls. One T-90 was in the process of turning to engage the Americans that had suddenly crested the rise when it was struck. The sabot round ripped through the vehicle's right side road wheels and drive sprocket. The tank lurched to a halt and the hatches were sprung by the impact. Before the Abrams could load another round and fire again, the Russian tank's three-man crew appeared, scrambling from within the steel hull. They climbed from the stricken vehicle with their hands held high in surrender, the driver's face dripping bright blood.

"Leave 'em be," the tank commander warned his gunner who had reached instinctively for the coax machine gun slaved to the Abrams turret. "They're out of the fight."

With the threat of the T-90s eliminated, the Abrams Battalion merged and turned to confront the advancing T-72s that were driving hard towards their flank. The T-72s were a danger to the American Abrams only if the Russians could close the range and target the vulnerable side and rear armor of the Abrams. The Americans first priority was to turn to meet the danger, presenting the thick armor of their front hulls to the enemy, and then reversing to keep the enemy at arm's length while the American tank's superior firepower and high-tech munitions could gain the advantage.

There was no time for parade ground formations. The closest American tanks to the advancing Russians simply pirouetted in the mud and reversed at high speed, firing on the run.

The Russians began to suffer. The sophisticated fire control gear aboard the Abrams tanks and the Cadillac Gage Gun Turret Drive and Stabilization Systems made for accurate targeting of the T-72s despite the undulating mud-churned ground. Four T-72s were destroyed in quick succession, each one marked by a fireball and rising column of black oily smoke. The Russian tankers fired back, doing little damage. An Abrams slewed sideways when it took a direct hit to its left-side running gear and two Abrams were struck flush on the turret, but the thick reactive armor deflected the enemy rounds and they whanged off into the distance.

Still the Russians bravely advanced. Two more T-72s were destroyed and then the tanks of Comanche Company added their considerable firepower to the uneven fight.

The Abrams crews fought with the cold-blooded ruthlessness of men who had endured the hell of enemy fire during their headlong charge and now faced an inferior and outnumbered enemy. They worked in the tight confines of their steal beasts like automatons, fear replaced by vengeful fury, their movements a testament to their training. One by one the Russian T-72s were destroyed until the surviving enemy MBTs could simply not endure any more. The first enemy tanks halted, and then began to reverse, popping off smoke to conceal their flight. Two Russian Su-25 'Frogfoots' overflew the battlefield, hoping to slow the American armored attack, but it was too little, too late. Allied fighters flying high overhead had air superiority. The 'Frogfoots' were engaged by Allied SAMs five miles behind the battlefront and shot from the sky even before the circling F-16s could vector to attack.

As the enemy tanks began to withdraw behind more smoke, Russian artillery fire streaked across the sky and plunged down through the blanket of smoke, falling indiscriminately across the expanse of the low valley. Some rounds landed in the Oder River, throwing up great watery eruptions. Other rounds landed amongst the fleeing Russian troops on the west bank who were trapped and traumatized with no route across the river. More rounds landed amidst the Abrams and T-72s, some of them exploding into huge white clouds of smoke while others exploded into fireballs and shrapnel fragments that thrashed against the hulls of the tanks like thrown gravel but did no damage.

The Russian flank collapsed.

"Get after them!" Colonel Zimmermann shouted at the monitors. "Push them back. Push! Push!"

One moment the Russian T-72s had been closing on the Abrams still ferociously willing to take the fight to the Americans. The next moment they were in full retreat, their flight hidden by a dense pall of smoke. The sudden artillery barrage was a concession, Zimmermann understood. The Russians had surrendered the battlefield and now were merely trying to turn the valley into a corridor of death the Americans would be reluctant to fight through. Zimmermann was having none of it. The Russian tanks had been defeated and now the American Colonel sensed the entire enemy flank was teetering on the verge of collapse.

Zimmermann bellowed orders across the Battalion net for the Abrams to continue their drive south, and then patched a call through to Brigade to request ground attack aircraft. "We've got the bastards on the run," he snarled, caught up in the elation of triumph. "Now I need some Hogs in the air, pronto, god-damnit!"

*

Wolf and Elway stood together at the eastern edge of the town, each lost in their own private thoughts as below them the Abrams tanks turned the western bank of the Oder River into a slaughterhouse.

A sudden rumble of heavy gunfire to the north made Elway turn in fresh alarm. He searched the skyline, peering through the haze that hung over the battlefield until he saw fresh blooms of smoke in the distance.

"The Leopards," Wolf said with satisfaction. "They're rolling up the Russian flank."

The German spearhead had struck home against the severed northern edge of the enemy's line. For several minutes the fighting to the north flared and flashed like far-away artillery fire and then the skyline seemed to shiver. Elway continued to watch. There was movement in the distance, still miles away and largely hidden by the skeins of smoke. He reached for binoculars and peered intently. For several long minutes he saw nothing, but then a new sound emerged; a rumble of heavy engines that trembled the air.

The 203rd Panzer Battalion appeared, first as a cloud of dust and shuddering noise, then as a mass of blurred, wavering movement. Finally individual tanks emerged through the smoke, streaked and ravaged with the battle-scars of their triumph. Karl Wolf allowed himself a cold smile of satisfaction.

It was clear now that there would be no more Russian attacks on Kleine Grenzstadt. The enemy were in chaotic headlong retreat; men, trucks and equipment log jamming the pontoon bridges as the broken remnants of the Russian Army's northern flank crumbled.

The allied tanks surged southward and added to the Russian panic, breaking through columns of retreating canvas-covered trucks around the town of Schwedt and tearing them to shreds with machine gun fire and HE rounds. Two A-10 Thunderbolts screamed low overhead and strafed one of the pontoon bridges. A BMP-1 exploded into flames and dozens of retreating Russian infantry were flung into the river and swept away.

Wolf watched the slaughter with grim satisfaction. Elway thought about all the men and women of Bravo Company who had sacrificed their lives to affect this victory.

"The irony," he turned and caught Karl Wolf's eye, "is that my Colonel wanted to surrender to the Russians just before you attacked in the woods. We had destroyed the first Krasukha and the enemy were overwhelming us. He turned to me on the edge of the riverbank and insisted we surrender. That was how he received his wound; he was raising his hands. In the aftermath of this battle, he'll probably get a medal for valor. And what do we get..?"

Karl Wolf smiled, but there was no humor in the expression. He faced Elway and the two men shook hands in farewell. "We don't soldier for medals, you and I. We're professionals. But maybe one day an author will write a book about your story and the world will discover what took place here. And if not," the German officer shrugged his shoulders as if to suggest such things were fanciful and not of any consequence, "then we will forever have the satisfaction that comes from a job well done and a mission successfully completed. It's all the reward a real warrior should ever expect."

Author's Note:

The town of Glauben Sie Stadt exists only in my imagination. There is no such town in Germany. In fact, the name 'Glauben Sie Stadt' loosely translates into English as 'make-believe town'. Similarly, the town of Kleine Grenzstadt is fictitious. The name in English loosely translates to 'small border town'.

I hope readers will forgive this small embellishment.

Acknowledgements:

The greatest thrill of writing, for me, is the opportunity to research the subject matter and to work with military, political and historical experts from around the world. I had a lot of help researching this book from the following groups and people. I am forever grateful for their willing enthusiasm and cooperation. Any remaining technical errors are mine.

Jill Blasy:

Jill has the editorial eye of an eagle! I trust Jill to read every manuscript, picking up typographical errors, missing commas, and for her general 'sense' of the book. Jill has been a great friend and a valuable part of my team for several years.

Jan Wade:

Jan is my Personal Assistant and an indispensable part of my team. She is a thoughtful, thorough, professional and persistent pleasure to work with. Chances are, if you're reading this book, it's due to Jan's engaging marketing and promotional efforts.

Dale Simpson:

Dale is a retired Special Forces operator who has been helping me with the military aspects of my writing since I first put pen to paper. He is my first point of contact for military technical advice. Over the years that he has been saving me from stupid mistakes we've become firm friends. The authenticity of the action and combat sequences in this novel are due to Dale's diligence and willing cooperation.

Dion Walker Sr:

Sergeant First Class (Retired) Dion Walker Sr, served 21 proud years in the US Army with deployments during Operation Desert Shield/Storm, Operation Intrinsic Action and Operation Iraqi Freedom. For 17 years he was a tanker in several Armor Battalions and Cavalry Squadrons before spending 4 years as an MGS (Stryker Mobile Gun System) Platoon Sergeant in a Stryker Infantry Company.

Jon Bernstein:

Jon Bernstein was already a published author with two books written on the AH-64 Apache helicopter when he commissioned into the US Army as an aviation officer in 2005. Jon flew both AH-64A and D models with 1-104th Attack Reconnaissance Battalion, Pennsylvania National Guard until 2012 and had 500 hours of Apache flight time. Jon is currently the Arms & Armor Curator at the National Museum of the Marine Corps.

I'm indebted to Jon for his expertise. He guided me through the technical aspects of the Apache's combat procedures as I was writing the tense attack scenes that preceded the book's climactic tank battle.

Facebook: https://www.facebook.com/NickRyanWW3
Website: https://www.worldwar3timeline.com

Made in the USA
Middletown, DE
18 August 2022